THE DAY OF THE JACKALOPE

ELDRITCH BLACK

Beware the rabbits!

Eldritch Black

The Day Of The Jackalope

PUBLISHED BY:
Eldritch Black
Copyright © 2019

http://eldritchblack.com/

All rights reserved.
No part of this publication may be copied, reproduced in any format, by any means, electronic or otherwise, without prior consent from the copyright owner and publisher of this book.
This is a work of fiction. All characters, names, places and events are the product of the author's imagination or used fictitiously

CONTENTS

I

THE MAGIC COIN

I t was a quiet, cool gray morning and the clouds were so low they seemed to scrape the treetops. It was summer, but I supposed strange weather like this was just the way it was living on Whidbey Island, or Weirdbey Island as me, Zach, Emily and Jacob now called it.

I'd been pulling weeds for what seemed like hours and my hands were caked in dirt. The back of my neck itched from mosquito bites, or whatever evil little bugs were sneaking up on me and sucking my blood.

Weeding wasn't really how I wanted to spend my day but mom was paying pretty generously by her standards. With the money I was making, I figured I was about five percent closer to getting the new laptop I wanted, plus mom was happy that it was getting done.

Besides, I wasn't missing out on anything big, things had pretty much stalled with our investigations. We'd spent the previous week searching for the Saratoga Sasquatch but the only thing we'd stumbled across was mud, brambles and horse apples. The lack of results had been frustrating, but I'd enjoyed hanging out with my new friends.

What I wasn't happy about was our super-creepy neighbor, Mrs. Chimes. She'd just driven by our house in her long, shiny chocolate-brown car and it had slowed as she'd spotted me. Her window had creaked as it had slid down and I'd waited for her to say something, anything. But she'd simply watched as I'd pulled out a handful of knotty weeds and a slow grin had spread over her wizened face.

"Morning," I'd called to break the awkward silence.

"Greetings!" she'd replied, and then she'd nodded slowly, like we'd shared something between us before driving off. It had been freaky, but apparently freaky was the norm on Weirdbey Island.

I was about to put on some music to distract myself when two shadows fell over me. One was stocky, the other so long it almost reached the edge of the house. A pang of dread slithered through me as I turned, already knowing who was there.

Jamie's stupid eyes gleamed with mockery. Beside him was his new friend; Marshall Anders. Marshall was a tall boy with a shaved head, dull, almost dead eyes and a face as craggy as the moon.

"The weed's weeding." Jamie sounded pleased with his insult.

"Yep," Marshall agreed. He smiled, but it only lasted a second. It was like he was trying to hide it and the way they stood made them look like they were up to something.

I ignored them and started working on the flower bed near the driveway, where I could keep an eye on them. I didn't want to turn my back on Jamie, not while my parents were out. "I've got stuff to do," I said as they continued watching me.

"Let's leave him to it," Jamie said.

I tried to hide my shudder. Something was definitely up; there was no way he'd leave me alone, not that easily. No,

Jamie liked to take his time torturing me, like a cat toying with a mouse.

"Gardening's no fun," Marshall said. "I had to weed my uncle's garden last month. It nearly broke my back." He leaned on the fence and gazed down at me. His face was almost... friendly? "You know, there's easier ways to get money, right?"

"Like what?" I asked. Right away I knew I should have kept my mouth shut. But it was too late, Marshall and I were officially having a chat.

"Like..." Marshall narrowed his eyes, as if deciding whether to tell me something. There was a long pause, and then he said, "like spending five cents and getting a dollar back."

Jamie sighed. "It's probably not working anymore." He pulled his hand from his pocket and his palm was full of shiny dollar coins, like the kind we used to get when we'd lost a tooth. I'd never seen so many in my life.

Marshall checked his phone. "Naw, it should be working again by now. We just needed to give it a rest. Its been at least an hour since the last time we tried it."

"Tried what?" I asked, unable to stop myself.

"The statue," Marshall replied as he pulled a handful of golden dollar coins from his pocket too. "See, I told you, it wasn't a trick." he said to Jamie, "I've still got all mine. They're real." He took one and bit into its side like people did in the movies. "You want some?" he asked me.

"Hey!" Jamie elbowed him in the side. "You said we weren't supposed to tell anyone and now you're bragging about it to this fool."

Marshall shook his head and studied me once more. "He's not so bad, are you?"

I shrugged. I had no idea what they were talking about, but the money had my interest. Was he really going to share it? I knew the answer already of course, but I could dream.

Marshall glanced around the yard, leaned down even closer to me, and smiled like we were old friends. "Look, if I tell you a secret, do you promise to keep it to yourself? Because-"

"Don't tell him!" Jamie's tone was shrill and whiney.

My curiosity was on fire. "Don't tell me what?"

Marshall glanced around again and lowered his voice. "I'm going to trust you, Dylan."

"Marshall!" Jamie protested.

But Marshall shook his head. "No, I'm telling him. There's enough for all three of us."

"You're as dumb as he is," Jamie muttered. And then Marshall rounded on him and he glanced away. Jamie was tough, but it seemed Marshall was tougher. I suddenly liked him more, despite those weird, dull eyes. Maybe he wasn't so bad after all. "Listen," he continued, "two houses down from here there's a statue of a lady. She's in the flowerbed on the side of Mr. Flittermouse's house."

"Mr. Flittermouse?" I asked.

"Yeah, he's just down the road. He's got a rusty old mail box with his name painted on the side right there next to his driveway. That's how you'll know you've got the right place. The plants in his yard are really wild and overgrown but you can't miss her."

"Who's the statue of?" I asked.

"His wife," Marshall said. "She died a couple of years back and he had the statue made to remember her by. But here's the interesting thing." He pulled a nickel from his wallet and held it toward me like it was something special. "This will sound crazy, but what you do is put five cents in her hands, close your eyes, and turn around three times. Counter-clockwise, it has to be counter-clockwise, you know what that is, right?"

I nodded. Of course I did.

"Good. So you spin around three times and after you're done, the nickel will turn into a golden dollar."

"You're joking, right?" I asked. "You expect me to believe that?"

My confidence melted as Marshall's eyes turned cold and dim once more. "Whatever. It's up to you, man." He shrugged but his face softened a little. "You know, I was just trying to do you a favor, but I suppose I didn't believe it when I first heard it either."

"Don't waste your time on him," Jamie said as he began to walk away, "time's money. Literally."

"I guess," Marshall said. And then he paused and flipped the nickel up into the air. It tumbled toward me and I managed to catch it without dropping it. "Give it a try, Dylan," Marshall called as he walked down the trail with Jamie, "what have you got to lose?"

I watched them go, half expecting them to turn and laugh at me, but they continued on their way. Jamie seemed angry, and I heard him mutter "What did you tell him for?"

Marshall answered but his voice was too low to hear as they vanished around the bend in the track.

I turned the coin over several times, inspecting it closely to figure out if they'd done something weird to it, but it didn't have a single suspicious mark on it. It was just a plain old nickel. I plunged the trowel into the earth and left it there as I glanced down the lane in the opposite direction. I'd never heard of Mr. Flittermouse, but then again I hadn't actually met any of our neighbors yet, except for Mrs. Chimes.

"What have I got to lose?" I shrugged, adopting Marshall's logic as I tried to persuade myself it was at least worth a try. I sighed, half expecting the worst but secretly hoping for the best as I set off down the trail.

A beam of golden sunlight broke from the clouds and

brightened the heavy green branches, as they cast dancing shadows over the ground. Squirrels chased each other across the limbs and a deer stood in the woods watching me. I considered going back to get our dog, Wilson, but he'd probably just be a hindrance, especially if things went wrong.

"Just a quick look," I told myself. "Then I'll get back to the weeding."

The first house I spotted was set back into the trees, but I could see its bright blue paint easily enough. I wondered who lived there and hoped it wasn't Mrs. Chimes, because that would mean she was our next door neighbor. I didn't like that idea one little bit.

Then I came to the next driveway. The pockmarked script on the battered old mailbox read 'Flittermouse'. I glanced along the curved gravel path but it vanished as it wound through the trees. And then my gaze fell on a sign posted on a tall hemlock just a few feet in from the road. It read:

'Trespass at your doom!'

"That doesn't sound very friendly." I glanced at my phone and considered calling Jacob, Zach and Emily, to see if they wanted to come with me. But then I realized, if I extended the invitation to investigate a magic statue that was handing out dollar coins and it turned out to be a hoax, I'd just end up looking like an idiot in front of them as well as Jamie and Marshall.

I rubbed the small of my back. It still ached from the weeding. I wasn't exactly looking forward to finishing the chore, but maybe I wouldn't have to... as unlikely as that was...

"This is so dumb." I started down the driveway, taking care to listen closely. It took a good couple of minutes of walking before I saw the house. It was covered in streaks of green and brown paint. "Who paints their house in...camouflage?" I mumbled.

It was too weird. I was about to turn and head back as fast as I could without running, when I saw a white figure through the trees.

My heart jumped. I stood absolutely still.

Then I realized it wasn't a person, it was the statue.

As I got closer I saw more details. It was a Japanese woman dressed in long robes and her hands were cupped before her. A sword rested at her feet and beside it was a lotus flower floating in an ornate bowl of water.

I listened hard. It seemed I was on my own. I glanced at the house again and realized there were no cars around. Hopefully that meant no one was home.

My attention shifted back to the statue. It couldn't hurt to check it out, could it? I wandered toward it, holding branches back as I stumbled through the tall grass, my eyes fixed on the stone woman. Something silver gleamed in her hand...

A coin!

Maybe Marshall and Jamie hadn't been lying after all.

"Wait," I whispered to myself as I slowed.

Someone else was there. Someone was watching.

I felt their eyes on me but they didn't make a sound. All I could hear was the distant drill of a woodpecker. I decided to go home. Fast.

And then I heard a whisper of movement, but before I could turn two hands clamped down on my shoulders, stopping me in my tracks.

FLITTERMOUSE

The hands clenching me smelt waxy and were streaked with woody colors. "Hey!" I yelled as I tried to pull away, but they held me firm. I kicked back and my sneaker struck what felt like a leg.

"Ow!" someone growled.

I spun around and came face to face with an old man dressed head to toe in camouflage. His face was smeared in green, brown and black and he'd even painted the few wisps of hair left on his head.

"Freeze!" he demanded as he waved his hands through the air and let out a slow, controlled breath. "That's right," he said, his voice creaky and gruff, but full of energy, "I move like the wind and dance like the lightning! You didn't see me coming and you never will. I am the tiger. I am the tiger!" He bellowed. He pointed his gnarled forefinger like a dagger. "Now, empty your pockets!"

"Why?" My heart was still racing, but I was more baffled than scared.

"Because I know a slippery customer when I see one, that's why. You have the look of a goat that's gobbled down more than his fair share of grass. Guilty, greedy, a gluttonous gazumper."

"What's a gazumper?"

He continued like he hadn't heard me. "You just wandered down my driveway as jittery as a turkey on Thanksgiving morn, and tried to sneak past me like a cat burglar on springs. But I knew you were on your way here before you even thought of it. My mind's as fast as a hurricane and sharper than a particularly sharp knife."

"I don't know that that makes sense," I said, before I could stop myself.

"Perhaps you're feeble minded? The name's Roscoe Flittermouse. You may have heard tell of me."

"Nope."

"Well my enemies have, you can count on that. And you are?"

"I'd expect you to already know who I am, especially if you knew I was on my way here before I even did." I replied. I didn't mean to be snippy, but I was angry. Mostly with myself for letting Jamie and Marshall dupe me. "Look, I'm sorry Mr. Flittermouse, I was just curious about your statue. I didn't mean any harm."

He studied me for a moment and gave a short sharp nod. "I see this is so, but I still require your name."

"Dylan Wilde."

"Ah, the Wildes. You've just moved into the old Prendergast place," he said, tapping his temple with his index finger as if this detail proved he possessed some sort of eerie mental super powers. "Now, I'm sure you'll understand that I'll need to have words with your parents, but other than that our business is concluded." Then his finger shot through the air like an arrow. "But listen and listen good; do not stray onto my land again. I prowl these woods with the stealth of a flea and the guile of an ancient otter."

"Are you..." I paused as I felt my cheeks reddening. And then I spat out the words as fast as I could. "Are you involved with The Society of the Owl and the Wolf?" He really seemed like he must be.

Mr. Flittermouse laughed theatrically. "Indeed I am not, but I know who they are. Our paths have crossed whilst fighting the darkness that prowls on our beautiful little island. And my oh my is it rising again."

He had my interest. "What do you mean?"

Mr. Flittermouse looked around before lowering his voice. "I mean the disappearances of course. Don't tell me you haven't noticed them."

"Disappearances?"

"People, tourists, locals. Vanishing in the dead of night like a forgotten rumor. Something rotten's a-roosting. Something terrible."

"What?"

Mr. Flittermouse shrugged. "How should I know? I spend my days guarding my trees."

"From what?"

"Theft!"

I glanced around. I couldn't see any tree stumps and I told him so.

"There are no stumps!" he said, as if I was the mad one. "No stumps, no displaced dirt, nothing but absence. One day a tree casts its shadow across the land and sinks its roots into the cool earth. The next it's gone as if it was never there." He leaned low. "I think she's taking them to her secret grove."

"Who?"

He laughed and tapped the side of his nose. "I'll not speak her name in the open. Let's just say she rings like a bell."

I thought about it. Chimes. "Mrs.-"

"Nope! Don't say it."

"She's taking trees and people?" Things were getting stranger and stranger.

"I never said she's the one stealing people. But I know for a fact she's got her grim sights set on my trees. No, the kidnapper, or peoplenapper to be more accurate, is a different force of darkness entirely."

"Right." I nodded. I hadn't heard of anyone going missing, and I couldn't see any evidence that his trees had been taken either. He was as mad as a box of frogs, it was as simple as that. "Look, I'm sorry I wandered up your driveway. It won't happen again."

"It better not. Now off with you, vamoose, scram!" Mr. Flittermouse lunged forward and pointed toward the road.

I stumbled through the undergrowth. When I looked back, he'd already gone. I wasn't surprised.

By the time I got home, Mr. Flittermouse had somehow gotten to my house and told my mom everything that had happened. She stood in the yard, arms folded, her face reddening, which was never a good sign. Jamie's head poked from the window behind her. He beamed a big cheesy grin at me. I ignored him.

"Well?" Mom asked.

"Erm, did, er, Mr. Flittermouse-"

"Yes. He kindly stopped by and explained you'd been interloping on his sacred earth. Those were his exact words."

"Look, I'm sorry. I just..."

"Just what?"

"I was just looking for something?" I tried to ignore Jamie as he mimed laughing behind mom. She spun around, as if sensing his stupidity, but by the time she'd turned he'd vanished.

"So what exactly were you looking for? And why?"

"I heard there was something in Mr. Flittermouse's garden... I don't know."

"And who exactly told you there was *something... I don't know* in Mr. Flittermouse's garden?"

"Just someone." Despite my anger I had no intention of snitching. For one thing, Jamie would make my life miserable once he caught up with me. For another, I didn't want his creepy friend Marshall on my case either.

"You're too easily influenced, Dylan. You need to learn to think for yourself." Mom's tone was softer now.

I nodded. "Sorry."

"Well, you've been warned. And if I hear you've been wandering onto other people's properties again, I'll ground you. Is that clear?"

I nodded again, like one of those toy dogs people put in the back window of their cars.

"You've got to be more careful, Dylan. There are strange people in this world. Do you understand me?"

Truer words were never spoken. "I do. Sorry, Mom."

She glanced at the garden where I'd dug out the weeds. "You did a good job. Now go inside and wash your hands, okay?"

I did as she said and refused to meet Jamie's eye as he watched from the doorway of his room. "Sucks to be you, Dylaboo!" he whispered.

Yeah, but only when you're around, I thought to myself.

I cleaned up, flopped down on my bed and read. After a while Wilson wandered in and tried to wash my feet. "What's up, boy." I scratched his ear and was thinking about taking him for a walk when the phone rang. A moment later Jamie shoved my door open and hurled the phone at me. "It's one of your idiot friends,' he said, loud enough for whoever was calling to hear.

"Your brother's a jerk," Zach said, as I answered the phone. "I should probably challenge him to a duel or something."

"You'd lose," I said.

"Maybe, maybe not. Anyway, that's not why I'm calling." I could hear cars and the distant squawk of gulls as he paused.

"So what do you want?" It seemed like it always took Zach forever to get to the point whenever he phoned.

"Uh, I just heard some very interesting news... We're heading over to the beach in Langley. You've got to get over there right now and meet us!"

"What is it?" I sat up fast. Wilson scrambled across the floor.

"Someone said they saw a mermaid, Dylan. A mermaid!"

❧ 3 ❧

THE WATCHERS

The breeze riffled my hair as I cycled through town, zipping past the parked cars. Langley was quiet, probably because it was a weekday and the gray sky carried the threat of rain.

My wheels juddered as I shot down the slope leading to the beach and passed by a bunch of people standing in a rough circle on the grassy path. I wondered if they were whale watchers, then I thought they might be looking for Zach's mermaid. Not that I was totally convinced it was real. But they weren't looking at the beach; they were looking at each other. Weird.

"Hey!" I hit my brakes as two rabbits darted in front of me, one fluffy and orange, the other speckled gray. They didn't even hesitate and with a sharp thrust of their hind legs they leaped over the long grass and vanished into the brush. I'd seen loads of them around town in the past week and I'd kept meaning to ask the others where they'd all come from.

The question slipped from my thoughts once again as I spotted Zach and Emily standing at the shoreline. Zach was pointing into the sea as the wind whipped along and sent his hair snaking up over his head. He lifted the bulky old fashioned camera he'd taken to wearing around his neck and started snapping away. I had no idea why he didn't just use his phone but he never seemed to do anything the normal way.

Something dark moved in the water. A head? Was someone swimming? No. I could see a tail...

I dropped my bike. "What is it?" I called.

Zach turned and grinned. "That's the hundred million dollar question."

The tide was coming in fast and the wind made the water choppy and white capped, causing the thing floating out there to sink below the waves. Whatever it was, it seemed lifeless. Dead. I shivered.

Shhhhhhh

I turned as Jacob shot toward us on his mountain bike, which always made mine look like a filthy relic. "What is it?" he asked as he leaned his bike on its stand and adjusted his glasses.

"A mermaid," Zach said, "I think..."

"It's not a mermaid," Emily said to Zach, her tone irritable, like she'd been telling him the same thing over and over. Her arms were folded tight, and she rolled her eyes as she glanced at me and Jacob.

"*It's not a mermaid,*" Zach repeated, mimicking her voice until she elbowed him in the ribs.

"Whoa!" I said as a wave lifted it up and I caught a glimpse of long blonde hair and a shadowy face. Then a great silvery tail splashed behind the creature. For some reason the thing, whatever it was, was wearing a blue T-shirt.

It vanished under the rolling waves then bobbed along and washed up on the beach before us.

"Ugh!" Emily held a hand over her nose and mouth.

"Oh man, that thing stinks! I gasped.

"It's dead..." Zach said, "poor thing!"

"It can't be dead," Jacob said with a sigh. "It was never alive. Not in its current form, anyway." He gingerly placed his foot on the side of the body and rolled it over, causing Zach to scream even louder than Emily.

I stared with horror into its monkey-like face, as scales slipped from its body and glittered on the sand. The logo on the T-shirt read, 'Bobby Spigot's Fish n' Chip Haven!"

"What the-" Zach's words tailed off as he stared down, stupefied.

"Ever hear of the Fiji Mermaid?" Jacob asked.

"Nope," I said.

Jacob held his phone studiously between his finger and thumb and began snapping photos. "They were sideshow exhibits back in the olden days. They were called mermaids, but really it was just a hoax, or what people into taxidermy would call a gaff. It's the top half of a monkey sewn onto the body of a big fish, but whoever made this one did a sloppy job. Look you can see the stitches by that fin."

"Why would anyone want to make something like that?" Emily's voice was riddled with disgust.

"Just as a curiosity I suppose. But I think this one's supposed to be some kind of marketing stunt," Jacob said as he examined the pictures he'd just taken. "It'll go viral alright, but for all the wrong reasons." He laughed.

"What should we do with it?" Zach asked. He sounded almost as disappointed as he was revolted.

"Chuck it in the trash so it's not littering the beach," Emily suggested.

"Or giving people nightmares," Jacob added.

"Too late. I'm going to have nightmares for the rest of my life," Zach said. He prodded it with his foot and it rolled over.

"Hey, it's really light!" He nodded to Emily. "Grab it by the tail Em, and we'll get rid of it."

"Ha! Why don't you grab it by the tail?" Emily asked, glaring back at him.

Zach looked over to Jacob and I, sighing like a world-weary old man as we shook our heads no. "Produce the coin of fate if you would, coin master," he said to Jacob.

Jacob dipped into his pocket and pulled out the quarter he kept for occasions such as this, and there were plenty. "Heads," he called as we made our bets.

After two more rounds Jacob proved the loser. He lifted the mermaid from the sand with care.

"Look, now you've got both heads and tails at the same time, Jacob," Zach laughed.

Jacob rolled his eyes. "Nice joke, Zach. But you're right," he said, "it's super light. The inside must be made of cork or something." Then he carried it across the beach, accepting his fate gracefully even as Zach took pictures and congratulated him on his bride-to-be.

"Enough," Emily said.

"It's never enough," Zach said, but he put his camera away and wheeled Jacob's bike along as we walked. Emily gave us all a wide berth as she cast sidelong glances at the creature. "I need something to take my mind off that thing," she said as we walked back toward town.

"Like what?" I asked.

"I dunno. Maybe we could get a milkshake. You owe me one, Zach, remember?"

He looked glum as he shrugged. "I guess. But are you sure you want to cash that favor in? It'll probably be lumpy or soured. Nothing's going right today. We can't get a decent lead on anything."

"Well, as far as I'm concerned the case of the Weirdbey

mermaid was just solved. So I for one feel motivated," Emily said to Zach and then they started sniping at each other as we headed toward the hill.

"Excuse me?"

I glanced up as a middle-aged couple approached us. They seemed startled and worried. Had they seen the mermaid? No, they weren't even looking at it.

"Hi," I said.

"Hi," the woman answered as she tucked her hair behind her ear and regarded us carefully. "We're looking for our mother." She held a phone up. The picture on the screen was of her and the man beside as well as an older lady with thin white hair. "Have you seen her?" she asked.

"No, sorry," I said.

The others peered at the image and shook their heads.

"Oh. Well thank you for your time," the woman said.

"It's her birthday" the man explained as he scanned the beach, "we brought her here to celebrate."

"To the beach?" Zach asked.

"No," the woman smiled, but it didn't last long. "To the island. We're staying at the motel, and when we went to meet up with her this morning she was gone."

"All her things are still there, her suitcase and purse," the man added, "but she didn't leave a note or anything. It's not like her to just disappear."

I thought back to what Mr. Flittermouse had said, about how people were going missing. I almost said something, but bit my tongue. It didn't seem like a good time to mention it.

"We'll keep an eye out for her," Zach said. "We're experienced at solving all kinds of mysteries, actually." He pulled a shiny black slip of paper from his pocket.

"What's that, Zachary?" Emily asked, her voice low.

"My business card. I got a good deal from the printers." Zach nodded to the man as he took the card.

"Zachary Brillion, Legendary Investigator, Pirate Slayer, Twenty-Four Hour Innovator. No job too large, small or medium." I... erm, well that's good to know. Thank you," the man gave a distracted nod as he pocketed the card.

"Yes, thank you for your time," the woman added. And then she glanced at the mermaid cradled in Jacob's arms and without another word they hurried away.

Jacob turned toward us. "I really need to get rid of this thing," he said holding the mermaid as far from his nose as possible.

They headed towards town. I was about to join them when I spotted something gleaming in the sand. I'd been collecting sea glass as well as oddly shaped pebbles and skimming stones for years, and it looked like I'd just struck gold.

I headed over to the patch of sand and pulled the glass out carefully. It was soft and glinted emerald green in my hand. Then I noticed a few more pieces nearby. I scooped them up, rubbed the damp gritty sand off and held them up to the bright spot of sun glowing through the clouds.

When I looked back the others were halfway up the slope. I placed the sea glass in my pocket, hopped onto my bike and cycled to catch up.

I was at the foot of the slope when I spotted the circle of people from earlier. They were still standing halfway up the grassy path. Now they were humming as they faced each other, and their strange grins were almost as creepy as the way they were gazing into each other's eyes.

And then a tall woman with big black glasses turned from the group and pointed right at me. "Come to us!" she called. "Now!"

✤ 4 ✤

SHAKES, BAKES AND
INTERSTELLAR CAKES

M y breath caught in my throat. The woman continued to point as if she'd just seen me doing something terrible. More of the strange people in the circle turned my way and their humming grew louder and louder.

I pedaled hard, dodging a huge rabbit as I shot up the hill. I slowed as I spotted Zach across the street, opening the door to 'Shakes, Bakes and Interstellar Cakes'.

I'd never been inside the diner before but I'd wandered by plenty of times. It looked retro with its black and white tiled floor, red tufted vinyl booths, and the vintage rocket ships hanging from the starry tiled ceiling. It seemed more like some bizarre movie set than a place to eat, which of course made it a favorite haunt of Zach's.

"Where'd you go?" Jacob asked as I stumbled through the door.

"I'll tell you in a minute," I whispered. There were people sitting nearby and I didn't want them to hear what I had to say.

"Let's sit by the window," Emily said, "we can keep an eye out for that missing lady."

I glanced across the road looking for any signs of the lunatics from the beach. It seemed like the coast was clear. Then I saw the *mermaid's* tail sticking out of a trashcan. Seconds later a woman and small child walked by. As the kid peered up at it, she let out a long shrill scream and her face turned the color of a ripe strawberry.

"Nice going, Zachary," Emily said.

Zach shrugged, "you're the one who told us to put it in the trash. Ah, here we go."

I looked up as a waitress zoomed toward us on roller skates. She had a tower of sparkling magenta hair and she was wearing contact lenses that made her eyes look like a cat's, or an alien's. I didn't ask why. We were on Weirdbey Island and that was all I needed to know.

"What can I get you?" she asked. Her pen hovered over her notepad like she had better things to do.

"I'll have the toffee and lime shake with bubblegum," Zach said.

"Popcorn and blackberry jam for me, please," Emily added.

The waitress turned her attention to Jacob. "Avocado and bacon?" she asked like it was his regular order. Jacob nodded and gave her a slightly embarrassed smile.

I gazed down at the menu which was decorated with stars, planets and UFOs. "Um, chocolate please." I waited until she glided off toward the kitchen then I put my elbows on the table and leaned in toward the others. "So, something really weird happened to me this morning. I wanted to tell you earlier, but with the mermaid and everything I never got the chance."

Zach wiggled the tips of his ears back and forth with his

fingers. "I'm all ears." Jacob snickered and Emily rolled her eyes.

I waited for a passing couple to shuffle by before telling the others about Jamie, Marshall and Mr. Flittermouse.

"He sounds nutty," Jacob said.

"Sure, but he said that people were going missing!" And then I described the weird people I'd seen chanting in a circle by the beach. I paused as the waitress delivered our milkshakes, took a long drink, and then continued.

"Could be a-" Emily paused as the lights in the diner flickered. "That's the second time today," she said.

"And we've already had three power outages in the last week," Jacob said. "One of them was when I was right in the middle of a boss fight. I was just about to finish the game and zap! It sucks. Anyway," he glanced back at me, "do you think the people you saw could have been whale watchers?"

"No, there was more to it than that. They just didn't seem like they belonged together, not in a group like that. They were all different ages. Some were dressed for work, you know shirts and ties and one was wearing a chef outfit. A few seemed like locals but some looked like tourists too," I said.

"And you think its got something to do with that missing woman?" Zach asked.

"Actually, she's not the only one I've heard about that's gone missing," Jacob said. "My mom said a whole family vanished last week."

"Where?" I asked.

"Out by Deer Lake. Poof! They just upped and went and that was the last anyone saw of them."

"This isn't good," Zach said as he spooned his milkshake. A dark look crossed his face. "It sounds like we've got a murderer on our hands. Maybe a strangler or-" his words tailed off as he gazed across the street.

We turned to see what he was gawping at.

Standing in a doorway across the way was a tall, whippet-thin man with wild mustard colored hair and a long lean face. His heavily shadowed eyes gleamed in his pasty-white face and I doubted he could have looked more sinister if he tried.

"He's watching them," Emily said. Ahead of the man were a pair of old ladies gazing into shop windows, oblivious to everything else around them. Then, as they crossed the road, he slipped from his doorway and strode after them.

"We should follow him," Zach said.

"Really?" Emily didn't sound convinced.

"I told those people I'd look for their mother," Zach said, "and this is our first lead. I think we've found our suspect." He drained his milkshake and wiped his foamy white mustache before burping loudly. "Sorry!" he said and covered his mouth as Emily winced.

"I think that's a dumb idea," Emily said as she continued to gaze through the window, "he looks like bad news."

"Yep" Jacob agreed, "I definitely don't want to get on his wrong side."

I shrugged as Zach glanced at me. "I think it's probably best to leave him alone." All the talk of missing people and murderers was spooking me.

"Then I guess I'll be investigating this one on my own." Zach sounded upset, but he straightened his shoulders and added, "right." He marched off without a backward glance.

Emily sighed, Jacob shrugged, and I nodded as we finished our milkshakes and paid up.

I found Zach a few doors down, peering around a wall. I glanced past him in time to see the man following the two old ladies down a short passage. We started after them but then he turned our way and we froze.

"Interesting," Jacob said as he pointed at a snail stuck to

the shop wall, like it was the most fascinating thing he'd ever seen. "Will you look at that?" We joined him until the man continued around the corner and disappeared from sight.

We ran down the alley and peered into the next. The man had caught up with the old ladies and now he had his hand on their shoulders, like he was steering them. They spoke together like they were old friends.

"What's he doing?" I asked.

"Nothing good," Zach said as we watched him lead them to the parking lot. They paused beside an old van with a chipped mural of rabbits, colorful eggs and lush grassy flourishes that had been painted on its weather-worn side panels.

The man said something, and they laughed together. Then the old ladies climbed in through the back door of the vehicle. The man slammed the door with a bang, and leaped into the driver's seat. We watched as they sped away, leaving nothing but a haze of dark exhaust behind them.

Zach rushed over to the empty spot where the van had been parked and examined the area as if he knew what he was looking for. He gazed up the hill. "I guess the trail's gone cold for now, but at least we have a lead."

"I'm not sure we've got anything," Jacob said as he checked his phone. "Anyway, I've got to go home."

"Yeah, we should head back too," Emily said. Zach nodded distractedly as the ghost of a smile turned his lips.

"What are you grinning for?" I asked.

"We've got a mystery to solve. A proper case!" Zach clapped me and Jacob on the shoulders. "Let's meet up in the Towering Lair of Eternal Secrets tomorrow. We'll work out a plan."

I agreed, even though I wasn't convinced there was anything much we could do about the missing people. Plus the man with the mustard colored hair had been beyond creepy and I wasn't sure that getting involved with the situation was one of Zach's better ideas.

"See you tomorrow," Jacob called as he cycled away.

I said goodbye and headed to the store to pick up some stuff for my mom. As I cycled through town, I saw another cluster of strange people standing across the street. They gazed blankly at each other, like they were hypnotized.

Slowly, they began to turn my way. I cycled hard, soaring along the street and up the hill as fast as my bike could take me.

Things were getting seriously strange on Weirdbey Island.

5

BACK TO THE TOWERING LAIR OF
ETERNAL SECRETS

The next morning I found myself climbing the ladder to Zach and Emily's tree house. Or 'The Towering Lair of Eternal Secrets' as Zach called it.

"Hey Dylan." Emily and Zach said at the same time.

"More people went missing last night," Jacob said as I sat down, "a family of tourists from Connecticut, and a husband and wife from Spokane. No one knows where they've gone."

"Whoah. So I guess whatever's taking people isn't slowing down." I sighed.

We didn't have a plan, except to keep an eye out for the creepy man we'd followed the day before and to try and find out if he was behind the disappearances. We headed into town watching for anything suspicious but everything seemed normal. It was just another summer's morning in Langley, at least until Emily spotted the sinister old van.

We watched as it drove down Second Street and stopped outside the library. As we reached it, Zach leaned down and tied his shoelaces really slowly so we could watch the van without standing out too much.

A moment later the window slid down and the creepy man

threw a half-eaten piece of toast out onto the street. His mustard-colored hair still sprung from his head like wires and dangled over his ghostly face. Then, the back door opened and the old ladies he'd driven off with the day before slowly climbed out. They smiled as they glanced around, but their eyes were dim, almost cloudy.

"They're alive." Zach said.

"You sound disappointed," Emily replied.

"Of course I'm not. But..." he floundered. It seemed we'd lost our main suspect.

"Here!" the man called as he leaned from the van and handed the ladies a pile of flyers. "Go and find us some more drones."

"Drones?" one of the old ladies asked.

"I meant friends. *Good* friends. Friends seeking a new path. Now go!" He flapped his hand, shooing them away and they strode down the hill. We watched as he glanced at himself in the mirror and grinned, flashing his teeth. Then his face grew stony and he tried another smile.

"It's like he's practicing," Jacob whispered.

"Don't be down," the man murmured as his wild eyes locked onto their own reflection. "There's a better way! Oh do I have something special for you!" He sounded like an actor studying his lines. Then, he climbed out of the van, straightened his navy blue tie against his crisp white shirt and strolled across the street. He never even noticed us.

We followed as he walked up to the people coming the other way and spoke with them. Some looked happy to talk to him, others seemed annoyed and moved away from him fast, as if he was a feral dog.

"I wonder what he's saying to them?" I asked.

"We need to get closer," Jacob said as he adjusted his glasses.

The man stopped outside the old fire station as soap bubbles from a nearby machine swirled through the air around him. His head swiveled this way and that, scanning the street for people and as a group approached, he fixed another smile into place.

I froze as his gaze swept over us. The edge of his lips curled into a grimace, but then he glanced away, like we weren't worth a second thought.

"Hey," Zach called as he strode up to him, "what's happening?"

"What's happening?"

"You know, what's going on? Are you having a good day?" Zach asked.

The man peered at each of us and gave his head a quick shake. "Go away, ridiculous children."

"Sure, we'll go," Zach said, "but can we have a flyer?" He pointed to the leaflets clasped in the man's hand.

"No. They're for people."

"We *are* people!" Emily was outraged.

The man studied her for a moment. "Technically, perhaps. But not the types that interest me. Not one of you. You seem like meddlers. Now go and darken someone else's day."

"But-" Zach began.

The man grimaced and stepped toward him. He stomped his foot down right on the tip of Zach's toes. "Go. Away!" he said through gritted teeth.

And then his face lit up with a great beaming smile as he glanced toward a young couple strolling up the hill. They looked as if they'd just had an argument. "Greetings! Good day!" he called, his voice warm and bright. "And may I say it's about to become a much better one than you could ever have imagined." He turned his back on us, as if we weren't there. Then he spoke to the couple so quietly we couldn't hear him.

Zach massaged his toes and looked like he was about to say something very bad.

"Come on," Jacob said motioning for us to leave, "there's more than one way to skin a cat."

Emily grimaced. "I don't want to skin any cats."

"It's just a figure of speech, Em," Zach said, casting the man another angry look before he turned to Jacob. "What are you thinking?"

"We need to find those ladies who were with him. They had flyers too. If we can get them to hand one over, we can find out what he's selling."

"We don't know that he's selling anything," I said.

"Oh we do," Jacob said, "he's selling something alright. Trust me."

We circled the block until we found one of the ladies standing outside the tiny cinema. She squinted as we walked up to her. "Can I help you?"

"May we have a flyer?" Jacob asked.

She shook her head. "I'm sorry, these are for grownups. Although," she smiled and her eyes turned dreamy, "if your parents read them, maybe they can bring you with them when they go to see him."

"See who?" Zach asked.

"You'll find out," the old lady said, and winked. "Trust me, everyone will learn soon enough." She took a deep breath. "The extraordinary celebration is coming. Oh joyous joy!"

"Um, can I bring a flyer to my parents?" Jacob asked.

The old lady considered it before holding one out. "It isn't strictly allowed, but why not?" Her painted eyebrows rose on her wrinkled forehead. "Just as long as you promise to bring them to see us, so we can make sure they're a good fit." She patted the back of Emily's hand. "Although I'm sure they will be."

"Thank you," Emily said. We skipped off, turned the corner and hurried to the tiny park across the street.

Once we were settled on the bench, Emily unfurled the flyer so we could all see it. Twisted briars drawn in ink formed a border around the edge and the headline at the top was in bold black writing.

"Yes it's time! Come and greet your shining future!" Emily read in a dramatic voice. "The one and only Jepa Cloak - visionary, marveler of minds and healer of broken hearts is finally here. Make an appointment today with one of our associates and take the first leap toward a better life!"

"What kind of name is Jepa?" I asked, pronouncing it the same way Emily had, which made it sound French.

"I don't know," Jacob said, "maybe we can ask him ourselves. How do we set up an appointment?" He narrowed his eyes as he tried to read the small print at the bottom of the flyer.

"Apparently we need to speak to Mr. Carrot, whoever that is," Emily said.

"How much do you want to bet that he's the moron who stomped on my foot?" Zach asked.

"Yeah, he seems to be the ring leader," Jacob said.

"We already know he's not going to talk to us," I said.

"Yup," Emily agreed, "which means we need to find another way to meet Jepa Cloak."

My phone rumbled. I scanned Dad's message. "I have to go home and take care of our dog while my parents take my brother to the dentist. Apparently it's an emergency."

"Maybe all his teeth fell out," Zach said. He sounded hopeful.

"I wish." I was still furious with Jamie and now, thanks to his stupid teeth, I was missing out on the first interesting thing to happen around here for days. "Let me know as soon as you find out anything, okay?" I asked.

"Of course we will." Emily pulled her phone out of her pocket and waved it in the air.

I pulled my bike out of the rack, cycled back up the hill and was almost at the track to my house when I heard the hum of tires behind me. It sounded like at least three bikes and I turned, expecting to find Zach, Emily and Jacob, but it wasn't them.

Two boys and a girl raced behind me. They were all around my age or so. The boy on the left was huge with closely cropped hair and dull, squidgy eyes. The girl was tall and athletic looking. Something about her cold smile made me think of a fox.

And the guy in the middle... he was downright weird.

His thick brown hair swept down like a curtain and his big bushy eyebrows were raised, making his dark eyes look permanently surprised. "You!" he called, his voice deeper than it seemed like it should have been. "Come here!" He sounded like the kind of kid that was used to getting what they wanted.

There was no way I was stopping. I sped up and cruised right past my house; I didn't want them knowing where I lived.

"Stop!" the boy shouted again as the fox-like girl hissed something, but I kept going, leading them down the street and away from my home.

It was only as I shot around the bend that I realized I was heading out of town. And that the road ahead was a long rural stretch.

There'd be no one out that way, no one around to help me...

6

HUNTED!

I sped down the winding tree-lined road. The clicking of gears and rumble of tires seemed closer and closer. The girl drew ahead of the others. It was almost like she was coasting downhill, the way she easily outpaced them. She didn't look like she'd broken a sweat, and her eyes shone with excitement.

Soon, I was going to run out of steam, and when I did, they'd catch me.

"I told you to stop, you-" the boy in the middle slowed as he coughed and spluttered and the sides of his face turned redder than they already were. The boy beside him slowed too.

My legs ached and my chest felt tight, but I raced on. No cars came by, it was like the road was deserted. It was just me and them.

I glanced over into a familiar patch of woods. I'd been in there once before. It was the place we'd been chased out of by our enemies the Strimples. They were gone now, but the place was just as dark and creepy as it had been on the day we'd gone in there scouting for their lair. But what choice did I have? I couldn't keep up this pace. If I headed into the woods, I might at least be able to hide in the trees...

I cycled as hard as I could, turned and shot up the small sloped track.

Three sets of brakes squealed behind me. I glanced back as the two boys crashed into each other, but they soon untangled their bikes and turned their wheels to come after me.

The girl thundered up the slope, her eyes fixed on mine.

I plunged through the trees, my wheels rolling across the soft spongy ground as the branches whipped past and a thick scent of evergreens hung in the air. I doubled back toward town.

Voices called out behind me. I could hear one of the boy's growling rasps. The girl didn't say a word. I shuddered as I thought of her horrible, fox-like grin.

Where was she?

I plunged on until finally a glow of light revealed an opening in the forest. I started to slow.

If I left the cover the trees provided, they'd see me and I'd be back to square one...

Mud and pine needles flew up as I skidded to a stop by some huckleberry bushes. Stumbling in a panic, I chucked my bike into the brush, smoothed over the marks I'd made in the muddy ground with my foot and ran to hide behind a tree trunk.

My phone rumbled. I grabbed it, glancing at Dad's angry-looking message as I switched it to silent.

The voices drew closer. Seconds later the kid with the bushy eyebrows cycled past, followed by the other boy. They hadn't seen me. They growled like furious bears as they edged along the trail and stopped in the clearing ahead.

Where was the girl? My heart raced harder as I imagined

her cold, calculating gaze at my back. She was like a huntress, a cunning, ruthless foe. And I was a wounded animal lost in the trees.

I watched as the large kid clamped his phone to the side of his sweaty red face.

Then a phone rang beside me.

I froze.

"What?" the girl asked, her voice as clear as day.

The back of my neck turned to gooseflesh. I chanced a look around the tree.

She was right there!

"No," she whispered, "I can't see him. I was going to try and flush him out, but you just blew my cover. Big time." She hung up, slipped her phone into her pocket and cycled over to join them.

They gathered in a circle and glanced back to the woods. At one point it seemed like the kid with the bushy eyebrows' gaze fell right on me, but then he looked away.

"Go away. Just go," I whispered as I willed them to give up and move on.

After what seemed like forever they turned and cycled back to the road, their heads hanging like sullen hounds who'd failed to catch their quarry.

Who were they? And why were they after me?

I hadn't done anything to them. I'd never even seen them before! Were they friends of Marshall or Jamie? Had they sent them after me? It didn't seem likely.

Then, as I thought of Jamie, I sent Dad a quick message and got ready to ride home as fast as I could. But as I reached to pull my bike out of the bush, something crashed in the trees behind me.

Thump, thump, thump!

Whatever it was, it was coming my way, and fast. The footsteps were dull and heavy, and pounded the ground like an escaped gorilla running on all fours.

Cold snaking fear froze me and I couldn't move as the sound of snapping branches grew louder and louder.

❧ 7 ❧

'DANGER!'

The thundering footsteps boomed and the ground felt like it was shaking.

Thump thump thump!

A dark silhouette loped through the trees, faster than any animal I'd ever seen.

Long curved antlers arced over its head and its big brown eyes seemed to glow as they fixed on me. The creature skidded to a halt, spun around three times on its huge paws and turned my way. Its ears twitched and its nose wrinkled. It was smelling me.

It wasn't like any kind of deer I'd ever seen, but it seemed nearly as big as one. It looked like... it looked like a rabbit. A huge rabbit with antlers. It lifted a paw to its mouth. Then it shook its head, and I got the impression it was telling me it couldn't talk.

"Of course it can't talk," I muttered to myself as I stared at it, dumbfounded.

It jabbed its paw at its mouth again, glanced back toward where it had come from, then hopped over to me. The rabbit, or whatever it was, gazed deeply into my eyes then leaned down and dragged an antler through the dirt at my feet.

It was... writing!

"Danger," I said out loud, as I read its spidery letters. "What the-"

My words tailed off as something crashed toward us through the trees.

The creature turned back to look, gave me a quick, imploring gaze, and raced off.

Thump thump thump!

I watched, gaping in stunned shock and total disbelief as it vanished into the gloom.

Whatever was hurtling after us through the woods was getting closer.

A cold, sharp bolt of fear shot through me. I grabbed my bike, jumped on the seat and fled like it was the devil himself behind me.

MYRON DRAVEN

The next day, after breakfast, I cycled to Zach and Emily's house, ditched my bike and climbed the ladder to The Towering Lair of Eternal Secrets.

"Hey!" Jacob was perched on a tree stump, and he nodded to me as I reached the last rung of the ladder. I was sweating and my breath was heavy and ragged, but the breeze that swept through the window was nice and cool.

Zach lay in his hammock sketching an image of Mr. Carrot. He'd really captured his likeness, especially the dark shadows beneath his eyes and his wild, wiry hair.

"Hey, Dylan," Zach said as Emily climbed up behind me and pulled a lever that sent the dumb waiter trundling up. Once it had rattled to a stop, she removed a tray with her breakfast; a soft-boiled egg and thin slices of buttered toast for dipping.

First, I told them about the three kids that had chased me the day before.

"The big guy sounds exactly like Eugene King. That means the girl was Cora Crook and the other guy has to be Myron

Draven." Jacob face twisted in disgust. "He's the brains of the operation."

"What's his problem?" I asked.

"He's a bully," Emily said.

"And an idiot," Zach added as he set his sketchbook down. "And his parents are just as bad. No one likes the Dravens."

Emily raised an eyebrow. "Cora and Myron seem to like…"

"No one normal likes the Dravens." Zach cut in.

"What do you think they wanted?" I asked as I tugged at the long sleeves of my hoody. I felt nervous again. I didn't need more bullies on my case, not when I already lived with one.

"They probably just wanted to find out who you are," Jacob said. "Territorial freaks. Myron seems to think the whole island's his turf."

"And he hates us," Emily said. "Big time. Which means once he finds out you hang out with us you'll be at the top of his hit list."

"Hit list?" I swallowed hard.

"Yeah," Zach said, "King and Draven do most of the hitting. Especially King. Crook prefers stalking and mind games."

"Great." I gazed down at the rooftop below us. Another problem. Just what I needed.

"There's something else, isn't there? What happened." Jacob asked.

I nodded. "Yep. And it's really weird. Too weird. So weird I need you to trust me, okay?"

"Cool!" Zach sat up like a dog on its best behavior. "Weird's our jam, Dylan. You know that. Fire away!"

I told them about the chase through the woods. And then, as I described the creature that had bounded toward me, I saw Jacob give Zach a quick, puzzled look.

"A rabbit, with antlers?" Emily asked. She glanced to the sky like she was trying to imagine such a thing.

"A really big rabbit with antlers," I added.

"It's called a jackalope," Zach said.

"And they don't exist," Jacob added. "It must have been another scheme, like the mermaid. Was it wearing a T-shirt with a logo on it?"

"No." The sides of my face burned with irritation. "And it wasn't a marketing stunt. It was real. I swear it!"

"Okay. I believe you, Dylan." Jacob said. He adjusted his glasses as he studied me. "I always thought jackalopes were hoaxes, but at this point, anything's possible. Did you see what it was running away from, or where it went?"

"Yeah, kind of."

"Can you take us to where you saw it?" Jacob asked.

"I think so. But I was on the run. It was kind of dark in the woods and I was pretty freaked out so I'm not sure of the exact spot. But it wasn't far from the old cabin the Strimples were hiding out in."

"If we get to the general area we can probably find your tracks," Jacob said.

"But what about the murderer?" Emily asked, "we're supposed to be looking for him, remember? I think that's more important than a big rabbit, if that's what it was. No disrespect, Dylan."

I shrugged.

Zach sighed and ran his fingers through his hair, making it even more unruly. "I scoped out Langley this morning. There was no sign of the van, or Mr. Carrot. The whole town was quiet. The only things I saw were a couple of deer loitering right in the middle of First Street and a bunch of rabbits hopping all over the place without a care. Let's go and investigate Dylan's close encounter before that trail runs cold too." He opened an old trunk and pulled out his camera. "Maybe I can get some pictures," he added. "Imagine what a photo of a real life jackalope would be worth! At least a few hundred grand. That would definitely be enough to get my investigation business up and running, and then I could hire you guys to work for me. Starting salary, a thousand bucks a day. Sweet, huh! Are you in?"

"I don't want to rain on your parade, but I'm pretty sure you'd never get that kind of money for a picture of a jackalope. People will just think it's a hoax," Jacob said.

"Not if I can prove it ain't a fakey, Jakey!" Zach's eyes gleamed as he strode past me to the ladder. "To your bikes ladies and gentlemen" he called, "and don't dawdle."

WE FANNED OUT BELOW THE TREES AS WE SEARCHED FOR MY tire tracks from the day before. Zach kept us in a tight formation so we *wouldn't contaminate the crime scene* until Jacob pointed out there hadn't actually been a crime.

Then, finally, Emily found some tire marks and the diamond shapes in the treads were easy enough to identify as mine. After that it didn't take long to find the huckleberry bushes where I'd stashed my bike.

"Whoa!" Zach said, gazing at the ground.

There they were; the jackalope's paw prints, still fresh in the mud. They looked even bigger than I remembered.

"Awesome!" He snapped a few pictures with his camera and turned to me. "Stand here and point at the tracks. Look really surprised. Also, look proud and brave and maybe suck in your cheeks a bit or something. Okay?"

"What for?" I asked.

"For the media of course. This is going to put you on the map, Dylan."

"I don't want to be on the map," I said, "I just want to find out what's going on."

"Fine, but you should be aware that this kind of attitude toward fame could be your first step toward becoming some sort of bizarre recluse. So don't say I didn't warn you." Zach sighed. "Right, let's track the big fellow then."

"It might be better to try and figure out what it was running from, instead of where it was going," Jacob suggested.

We pushed our bikes along as we wandered through the trees following the trail of smashed branches, scattered leaves and heavy prints. Then I noticed gouges in the tree bark where its antlers had scraped them.

"Wait," Emily whispered, holding up her hand.

We froze, and then I heard the voices too. Daylight shone through the branches ahead and at first I thought we'd circled back toward the roadside. But then I saw the clearing. "Let's get a closer look," I said, my curiosity burning.

We leaned our bikes against the trees and slowly wandered toward the meadow.

The first thing I saw was a huge striped red and green tent on the far side of the clearing. Then the long, arcing strings of lights draped from the tent poles. They gleamed, dim and soft in the gloom, and for a moment it felt like Christmas had come early.

Twenty or more people waited outside the tent, but no one spoke or moved. They were like the strange groups I'd seen in town; their eyes blank and their smiles wide and creepy. Like robots that had been powered down.

"Look," Emily said.

I followed her gaze as Mr. Carrot emerged from the tent, his face stony and serious. He wore a black suit and picked at something on his sleeve as he strode to his van, which was parked in the shadow of the woods. Then he came back with a handful of flyers and passed them out to the waiting people.

Mr. Carrot's voice boomed over the hushed quiet. "We only signed up a hundred and seven yesterday. A hundred and seven!" He shook his head and the smiles on the people's faces faded. "The master's most displeased." He rounded on the group and glanced at them one by one. "Do you want a new life? Do you want the chance to fly like angels?"

They nodded quickly.

"Then get out there, do your part! Bring back fifty people each. I want at least a thousand people at tonight's event. And tomorrow; I want five thousand! We need those numbers for the eve of the extraordinary celebration. And I don't need to tell you we only have two more nights to reach our goal! Two nights!"

Mr. Carrot gazed at them for a moment more before turning to a young man with long blonde hair tied in a ponytail. He was the man we'd seen Mr. Carrot talking to the day before. Then as I glanced to his side, I saw the girl that had been with him. She looked just as lost as he did.

"Come with me, Daniel," Mr. Carrot said, "I've a special task for you. A *very* special task." He guided him to the tent and together they slipped through the opening, too fast for us to see whatever was hidden inside.

"We need to get a closer look," Jacob said, as if reading my thoughts.

"Yeah." I agreed. Not that I was happy about the idea. "I suppose if something goes wrong we can make a run for our bikes," I said. Living with Jamie meant I was used to making escape plans.

We crept through the woods and were almost in the clearing when we froze. A hushed voice spoke inside the tent.

It drifted out like a loud whisper but I could hear it clearly from where I stood.

I checked to see if the others had heard it too, but they were gazing ahead like deer in the headlights.

Yesssss, the voice whispered, *Come to me. Start your new life. Don't be afraid! Together we shall throw open the doors to a new tomorrow!*

Where was it coming from?

Suddenly, all my own thoughts slipped from my mind and it felt as if my head was completely empty. *That's right,* the voice whispered. Somehow it sounded as if it was lodged right between my ears. *Come to me,* it continued, *come now and let the transformation begin!*

You're so brave, Dylan, the voice in my head purred, *so stout of heart. You deserve better from this world, and you will have your heart's desire. You'll thrive underground with the others, you'll be so happy in your new home! A shining beacon of light to those around you. You have the strongest soul, Dylan. The strongest soul there ever was. Don't doubt, don't fear. Come to me, and bring your fine friends with you.*

I nodded. This was everything I wanted. I could bring Jacob, Emily and Zach with me and together we could start new, better lives. We'd be powerful beyond our wildest dreams...

The whispering voice stopped and suddenly I missed it, like I'd lost the most valuable thing in the world.

We were almost at the edge of the clearing when a terrible, burning itch spread across the back of my neck. It was horrible. Not the itch, but the way it dragged me from my soft comfortable trance.

I clapped a hand to my neck and felt the bump where a bug had bitten me and suddenly I remembered where I was. And who I was. And what had happened. I turned and watched as my friends shuffled like zombies toward the tent. Zach was the closest. I reached out and pinched his arm.

"Ow!" He turned on me, his eyes cloudy and irritable.

"Wake up!" I pinched him again.

He glared but slowly his gaze softened. "What? What's happened?" he asked.

"I don't know... it's like you were in a trance. We need to wake Emily and Jacob too." I stumbled to Jacob and pinched his shoulder, while Zach did the same to Emily. They yelped and it took a moment for them to snap out of it. When they did, they shook their heads and stretched, like they'd just woken up.

"Did you hear the voice?" Emily asked as she gazed at the tent.

"Yeah," I said.

"Me too." Jacob shook his head again like he was still trying to clear it. He adjusted his glasses and gave the tent a worried glance.

"We need to get away from this place," I said.

Dylannn, the voice whispered again. I pinched the back of my hand and followed the others as they ran into the shadowy woods.

"After them!" The voice commanded, but this time it came from the tent instead of between my ears.

Five of the people standing by the marquee turned, broke from the crowd and raced toward us. Somehow, they knew exactly where we'd gone and as I turned back, I realized a bunch of the people that had been there were now missing.

Where had they gone?

"Run!" We sprinted through the undergrowth to our bikes. Zach was way ahead, Jacob by my side and Emily...

She'd fallen.

I ran back to get her and watched with horror as the

people that the voice had sent after us burst through the trees. Emily looked totally panicked as she glanced up at them. Before I could reach her, she sprang to her feet and caught up to me.

Jacob and Zach were already on their bikes and holding ours up by the handlebars. "Run!" Zach shouted.

Bushes crashed and branches whipped and snapped as the people spread out around us. And then, as we jumped onto our seats and started to take off, more appeared ahead.

They began to form a circle.

"Go! Go now. Bust through them!" Jacob said as he kicked down on his pedals. Emily followed him.

I cycled after them but the mob closed in so I shot off to the right where there were fewer of them. Two men leaped and stumbled after me, their hands grasping the air. I ducked as one grabbed at my hoody and only just made it past the other as he pounced at me.

Zach zipped through the trees ahead, his panicked cries echoing back my way.

Icy terror shivered down my spine as pounding feet crashed behind me in pursuit.

THE MIDNIGHT VISIT

We shot through the woods, jumping logs and pedaling hard as figures rushed towards us through the surrounding brush. We raced and raced for what felt like forever. Then we finally emerged from the trees and picked up speed as we flew down the road.

"I gotta stop!" Zach's tires screeched as he squeezed the brakes. I pulled over next to him and Emily and Jacob swooped up beside us. I took long heaving breaths. My head pounded and a deep ache throbbed though my legs.

"Did you guys hear that creepy voice too? What was it? What's going on?" Emily asked.

"I don't know," I said, "I thought it was just me, it sounded like it was-"

"Inside your mind," Jacob finished as he wiped the fog from his glasses.

"It said stuff that..." Zach stopped talking and a strange look passed over his face. It was almost hopeful.

"Did it say nice things?" I asked.

"He said I was going to be famous. *World* famous," Zach said, "and soon."

"He told me stuff like that too," Jacob said. But he didn't tell us exactly what the voice had said, and neither did Emily.

"We need help," I said, "we can't handle this on our own."

"You're right." Jacob sounded relieved I'd said it. "We should go to the police."

Zach sighed. "And miss the chance to solve the crime of the century ourselves? Think of the prestige! People would have to take us seriously. Imagine where solving a mystery like this could get us!"

"It'll get us a one way ticket to zombieland, just like the others! Think about this, Zachary," Emily said, "whatever's in that tent was able to get right into our minds. It's bad news, Zach, *really* bad news."

He seemed to consider it, and I saw him shiver before he said, "I guess you're right."

We rode back to Langley and stopped outside the small brick police station. There was only one cop on duty; an older man who was busy staring at his phone screen. He glanced up as we bustled in and looked almost irritated, as if we were interrupting him. But then he seemed to compose himself and he smiled. "Everything okay, kids?"

"Nope," Zach said, "but you probably don't need us to tell you that. You know about the murderer, right?"

"Murderer? Here? Is that right?" The cop shrugged and his eyes flitted back to his phone before settling on us once more, like he was torn between two things.

"Well, we don't actually know if anyone's been murdered," Emily added, "but we do know that people are going missing. And we think we know who's behind it."

"Who?" The cop sounded like he was trying to take us seriously but he wasn't doing a very good job.

"Jepa Cloak! The marveler of minds," Zach said, "we think him and his creepy followers are kidnapping people."

"No one's missing, son." A slow, happy smile crept over the cop's face. "Everyone's found a new way. Including me."

"But they have a tent out in the woods, and these–" Emily began.

"We know about the tent, miss," the cop said, "and there's nothing to worry about, I can assure you. Those people have all the proper permits to be there, and I for one thank the great one that they're here!" His eyes gleamed as he looked at each of us. "Have you been to see him yet?"

"The fortune teller?" I asked.

"Yes, the amazing Jepa Cloak!" He laughed. "Trust me, if you haven't, you're in for a real treat!"

"But–" Jacob began.

"No buts!" the cop said. "Now, if you'll excuse me I need to pick out my new boat." He turned his phone toward us and nodded to the picture of a yacht he'd been looking at. The price of the boat was off to the right and the number was so long it ran off the side of the screen.

"I didn't realize cops could afford stuff like that," Zach said. He looked excited. "How do I sign up?"

The cop grinned, but as I looked closer I saw his eyes were dull and distant, almost like he was daydreaming... like he wasn't really there. "Oh, we don't get paid enough to buy one of these beauties. No, this is coming from my big win."

"You won the lottery?" Emily asked.

He pulled a ticket from his pocket. "Not yet, but I will. Next Saturday. Five million!" The paper in his hand looked blank from where I stood.

"How do you know you're going to win?" I asked, but I had a feeling I knew exactly what he was going to say.

"The amazing Jepa Cloak told me, that's how. Now," he waved his hand toward the door, "if you'll excuse me I've got plans to make."

"But what about the missing–"

"No one's missing, young man. I told you that already." He gave us an irritable look. "Right, as I said, I'm busy."

Emily yanked Zach out the door of the station and Jacob and me followed. We stood outside on a patch of grass as the sun broke through the clouds and shone down on us. "So what do we do now?" I asked.

"We solve the problem ourselves. Like we should have done all along," Zach said, "The cops may know what they're doing with day to day stuff, but not when it comes to things like this. Not when it comes to..." he dropped his voice, "the supernatural."

I nodded and stared at my feet blankly. Jacob and Emily didn't say anything. I guessed they probably didn't want to get involved either, but it wasn't like we had a choice. I glanced up as a group of people walked by. Each one clutched a stack of Jepa Cloak leaflets in their hands and their faces were lit with creepy smiles. It was like the whole town had gone mad and we were the only sane ones left.

"We should head home," Emily said, "we're supposed to go shopping with Mom."

"I need to get home too," Jacob said.

So we said our goodbyes and I cycled off with Jacob.

It seemed there were more and more people standing in the streets staring as we zipped by. And there were rabbits everywhere. They hopped around nibbling the grass and weaved in and out of people's feet. Some even peered out from the flowerbeds and bushes like they were watching us.

"Later, Dylan," Jacob called as I cycled on.

"Later," I called back.

The sun vanished behind some clouds, matching my darkening mood. What was going on? It felt like the whole island had gone crazy! I wondered if the same thing was happening in the rest of the country, or even the world. Probably not, but what if it was?

I skimmed the news when I got home but nothing caught my eye. It was the same old same old, which meant all the trouble seemed to be focused right where I was, on Weirdbey. It figured.

IT WAS JUST AFTER MIDNIGHT WHEN I WOKE. I SAT UP AND gazed into the darkness as I tried to figure out what had woken me. I thought I heard Wilson bark, but it seemed to stop almost as quickly as it had started.

I thought about going back to sleep as fast as possible, but then Wilson growled again and I began to worry something was wrong. I opened my door and crept down the hall, hoping to see a light in my parent's room, or even Jamie's, but the house was completely dark. Everyone was asleep, but not me.

The top step creaked, so I moved to the side of the stairs and walked down as quietly as I could. I was almost at the last step when Wilson stopped growling.

Silence fell.

Something rustled against the window. It couldn't be falling leaves? Not in the middle of summer? My mind leaped to Mrs. Chimes. Was she out there doing whatever things dark witches do after midnight?

I shivered. Maybe it was Mr. Carrot...

Wilson scuttled from his basket and sat in the middle of the living room. He panted as I approached him and turned and stared at the front door, his ears high and straight.

"What is it?" I whispered.

He didn't reply. I wasn't really expecting him to but I wished he could have. Almost as much as I wished I didn't have to be the one to look outside to see what was lurking out there.

I peered through the keyhole but it was too dark to see anything.

There was no way I was opening the door, so I tip-toed to the window and drew back the curtain. My heart thumped like a booming drum as I half expected to find a pale face pressed against the glass.

It was clear. No witches, no maniacs. Just the trees and the dark, dark night.

But as I let the curtain fall, I couldn't help feeling like someone, or something, was out there watching. And whoever, or whatever it was, it wasn't good.

❧ II ☙

A RETURN TO THE DARK HOUSE

Wilson barked, and for a horrible moment I thought it was still the middle of the night. Then, as my eyes popped open, I was relieved to find the room filled with daylight. Wilson barked again and then I heard Jamie calling him. It sounded like they were out in the yard. Everything was okay, we were still alive.

I climbed out of bed and did my best to straighten down my hair. I yawned, still groggy, and winced as I remembered my dreams. They'd been more like nightmares after my creepy midnight encounter and I was surprised I'd actually managed to get back to sleep. I ate some toast before riding over to Zach and Emily's house. It might have felt like a normal day, if I hadn't known there was a tent full of lunatics down the road. I kept a watchful eye out for Mr. Carrot's van as well as his freaky followers, but there was no sign of them.

As I thought of the tent, the memory of the strange voice returned to me. What if he was right? What if better things were waiting for us? It wasn't impossible, was it? I began to wonder if I should reconsider what he'd said... maybe we all should.

I shook my head. He'd been lying. He'd just said things I wanted to hear. It wasn't the first time I'd fallen for tricks like that thanks to Jamie's endless pranks. Nothing good ever came from lies, even when I wanted to believe them. *Especially* when I wanted to believe them.

A cool breeze rustled the leaves as I climbed the tree house ladder. It sounded like all three of them were already there. "It's only a matter of time," Zach said. He flinched as I clambered over the lip of the trap door, like he was expecting me to be someone else.

"Only a matter of time until what?" I asked.

"Until they find us," he replied. Emily and Jacob sat behind him watching as he paced along the wooden boards.

"Who?"

"The zombie people that chased us from the woods," Zach said, "who do you think?"

"Erm, technically they weren't zombies," Jacob said.

"You know what I mean!" Zach looked flustered and his hair was even crazier than mine. He looked like he hadn't slept, so did Jacob and Emily. I knew how they felt. "Anyway," he continued, "whatever you want to call them, they're going to be looking for us now. They know we're onto them. How long before one of us goes missing? Or all of us?" He gulped and glanced around again.

"We need help," Emily said.

"We tried that yesterday, remember?" Zach said. "The police are part of it!"

"One is," Jacob corrected. "He doesn't represent them all."

"What about the Society?" I suggested.

"What society?" Zach looked genuinely confused.

"The Society of the Owl and the Wolf. They're supposed to deal with stuff like this, right?"

"*Supposed* to, yeah," Zach said, "but they weren't exactly on the ball when Captain Grimdire showed up, were they? Not that any of us have even met them, apart from you."

"Maybe they're working undercover. Maybe that's why I haven't seen them around. Maybe they're investigating the tent right now," I said. It was a lame idea, and I knew it. The Society of the Owl and the Wolf seemed about as useful as a chocolate teapot, as my nan would say.

"I don't think anyone can help us." Zach cast another nervous glance down to the street as a car drove past.

"Well we won't know until we ask," I said.

"The house was totally empty the last time we went to see them," Jacob pointed out.

I'd never mentioned I'd gone back there. Mostly because I'd hoped I'd never have to see Mr. Ovalhide or his weird friends again. "Actually," I said, "I went by there and dropped off the book and map after we defeated Grimdire. There was a light on. Someone was home."

"When?" Emily asked.

"A couple of weeks ago."

"Well, I guess we should stop by again and take a look," Zach said. "Anything's got to be worth a shot right now."

WE SKIDDED TO A HALT BEHIND THE DUSTY CAR PARKED IN Mr. Ovalhide's driveway. It looked like it had been there for a while. The house was as dark and bedraggled as the last time I'd been there but now all the curtains were drawn.

None of us wanted to knock on the door, and each of us looked at the other like they should be the one to have to do it.

"It's time for the coin toss of doom." Zach turned to Jacob.

Emily gave a loud, impatient sigh, pushed past us and

rapped her knuckles on the door. A noise came from inside the house. It sounded weird, almost like a human barking.

Then, before I could step back, the door swung open and Mr. Ovalhide loomed over us.

I'd forgotten how tall he was; the crown of his balding head almost touched the top of the doorframe. He ran a hand over the few gray strings of hair left on his head and patted them into place. Then his pale blue eyes flitted over us. "I... achoo!" He barely managed to clamp the spotted handkerchief over his mouth in time.

"Achoo!" Someone else sneezed inside the house, as if in reply to him.

"Ah," Mr. Ovalhide gazed down at me, "it's you." He reached out to shake my hand but I didn't move. "Right, you don't want to catch this plague, I wouldn't either. Funnily enough, I was going to look for you. Then I was struck down with this illness," he continued. "But I wanted to thank you for taking care of the Penn Cove situation."

"The Penn Cove situation?" Zach said, "Oh right, I think you meant to say the horde of cursed pirates, the creepy murderous Strimples and the giant angry flailing octopus situation?"

"Yes, yes indeed. One of our members spotted you on the cove that night. They told us of your heroic bravery," Mr. Ovalhide said.

"What? While they watched and did nothing?" Zach asked. Clearly he wasn't impressed.

"But that's not why we came today. We're here about the missing people." Jacob interrupted.

Mr. Ovalhide glanced around before ushering us into his house. "That's not the sort of conversation that should be had... out in the open like this. Come in."

The others looked at me as if to say *are you serious?* I saw their point; the house was old and spooky and Mr. Ovalhide was definitely weird. But I'd been there before and he was one of the good guys, sort of. Plus, Zach and Emily had given their sister Violet the address of where we were going, just in case.

So slowly, and cautiously, we stepped into the darkened house.

12

THE FIRST MISSION

The house was furnished again. Sofas and chairs dotted the room and some had been pushed up against the faded green wallpaper. Most of the really weird stuff was back too. Zach stooped to examine the tiny statues of strange fearsome creatures that seemed to stand guard under a row of creepy paintings. Jacob stared at an image of skeletons dancing beneath a flying saucer. Emily gazed at a painting of a crowded market full of goblins, and then to the portrait of a vampire-like man whose eyes seemed to follow us around the room.

"Hey Cyril!" I said as the gray cat I remembered from the midnight garage sale, brushed against my shin. I paused and patted his head, even though it was his fault that I'd ended up in this whole mess in the first place. If I'd never followed him up the stairs...

"Achoo!" A woman jumped up from the sofa and strode toward us. She was almost as tall as Mr. Ovalhide, thin and willowy and her dyed orange hair was like flames against her black pajamas. "Cosmia," she nodded to each of us and then her gaze fell on me. "Monty told me what you did." Monty? It

63

took a moment to remember Mr. Ovalhide's name was Montgomery. "Pleased... achoo! To... achoo! Meet... achoo-"

"You?" Zach asked, finishing her sentence for her.

She smiled as she clamped a handkerchief over her nose. "So you're the one who showed up at my husband's ridiculous midnight garage sale." She gave Mr. Ovalhide an exasperated look and his cheeks colored.

"Um, that was me," I said. "My mom's an addict."

"He means a garage sale addict," Emily added quickly.

"Yep," Zach said. "And after that he met up with us and we saved the whole island. Without much help from anyone else. Actually, without *any* help."

Jacob flashed a sheepish apologetic smile, the same one I'd seen before when Zach had spoken up like that.

"I was away on business," Cosmia said, "but if I'd been here you'd certainly have been given more assistance than you were." She gave her husband another pointed look.

"Yes, we did rather leave you in the lurch," Mr. Ovalhide said, "and for that you have my sincerest apologies. After the Grimdire incident the Society disbanded. Sadly, we've all been forced to accept we're too old to be chasing things that go bump in the night. And none of our grandchildren seem interested in taking up the mantle. Indeed, most have moved off the island altogether."

"So what's going to happen now?" Zach asked. He looked worried.

"Well," Mr. Ovalhide sat beside his wife and gestured for us to take a seat on the other sofa. "That's why I was rather hoping to find you." He glanced at me as the cat jumped onto my lap, pinning me into place. "But as it happens, you've found us. I take it you've discovered things are going amiss once more?"

I nodded.

"The fact we've all found each other like this means it's meant!" Cosmia said and gave us a long, searching look.

"It certainly seems that way. We asked for help and the universe has provided," Mr. Ovalhide said. And then his smile vanished as he sneezed again. "Excuse me; this cold's a curse unto itself. And right in the middle of summer. But anyway, what do you think?"

"About what?" Zach asked, even though it seemed he knew exactly what Mr. Ovalhide was suggesting.

"About carrying on with the Society's duties," Cosmia said.

"So you're not real choosy about who joins," Jacob said as he adjusted his glasses and gave them a long, serious look. "Not to be rude, but I always thought secret societies were a lot tougher to get into."

"Beggars can't be choosers," Mr. Ovalhide said, "and we're beggars alright."

"You know we're just kids, right?" Zach said. "Don't get me wrong, I'm totally in, of course I am. I'm so in that I was already in before you offered. This is exactly what I need to kick-start my career. But you should probably know we're already in a society." He glanced at Jacob, "not that we've gotten that much done since we started it, so it shouldn't be a conflict."

"We didn't get *anything* done," Jacob said, "apart from reading old library books and cycling around looking for stuff that wasn't there."

"Well," Mr. Ovalhide said, "I won't lie. Adults would make more suitable replacements, especially considering the danger involved. But..." his words drifted off.

"But no one believes us," Cosmia finished. "Folks barely see what's before them these days. No sense, no imagination, most are as blind as bats! You could put a ten foot neon belly dancing dragon right in front of them and they'd refuse to see it. Well, the majority at least."

"And not being open to such things definitely puts people at a disadvantage. Imagine when the day arrives and they have to face down a feral werewolf, or a shrieking banshee," Mr. Ovalhide said. "This is why we were recruited into the Society when we weren't much older than you. Because we were still open to seeing the unseen, or imagining it at least. We helped our parents for years, and then, when they were too tired to continue the struggle, we took over for them."

"And now you want us to take over, but we won't get any help like you did?" Emily asked.

"Well you've already more than proven your mettle," Mr. Ovalhide replied. "You defeated Captain Grimdire, as well as the Strimples, and that was no small feat. But we'll understand if you're not interested."

"We're interested," Zach said, "well, I am. But we'll need help, in fact we need help now. Do you know why there are people going missing on the island? Do you know who's taking them?"

"I'm afraid not," Mr. Ovalhide said. "We sent the last remaining members of our Society to look into it and…"

"We haven't heard a peep from them since," Cosmia finished.

"And that was only a few days ago. It's alarming" Mr. Ovalhide continued. "We'd investigate it ourselves but…" his face screwed up and he sneezed again, and the handkerchief in his hand billowed as if it was in a hurricane.

"Achoo!" His wife cried after him.

"We'll look into it," Zach said, and then glanced at each of us in turn.

Jacob and Emily nodded solemnly, and I did the same. I wasn't sure I wanted to join The Society of the Owl and the

Wolf, but I kept those doubts to myself. Because as I thought back to the picture of the old lady who'd gone missing, and the others who had vanished, I knew we had to do something. Someone had to.

"Good!" Mr. Ovalhide clapped his hands so hard the cat sprang from my knee and proceeded to pad out of the room with a scowl. "This will be your first mission as owls and wolves! But before you go, you must tell us everything you know about this most mysterious case."

❧ 13 ❧

FUBBABADDABOOBA

No one else spoke up, so I cleared my throat and told the story. I started with the people who'd asked us to find their missing mother, described the creature I'd seen in the woods, and wrapped up the story with the spooky voice in the tent.

"You don't say," Mr. Ovalhide said. He leaned forward, his hands on his knees. "And this voice whispered in your minds rather than your ears?"

We nodded.

"Whatever it is, it's using powerful magic," he continued, "very powerful magic indeed."

I'd always thought magic wasn't real, that it was something that just existed in stories, but I'd found out how real it was when we'd come face to face with Captain Grimdire. Still, it seemed weird hearing an adult talk about it, like it was as normal as electricity.

"Are you sure it's magic?" Jacob asked, "I mean, we saw equipment outside the tent. Some of it definitely looked like AV stuff and there were speakers, or amplifiers."

Mr. Ovalhide nodded. "You're quite right, it sounds like

there's definitely some form of technology involved in this strange affair. But I feel that, at its heart, there's magic afoot. *Dark* magic. However, if they're using amplifiers then there's got to be a signal of sorts. And if there's a signal, it can be disrupted and we may well know someone who can help with that." He turned to his wife.

"Oh, you mean *her*," Cosmia said doubtfully.

"Who?" Zach asked.

"Ophelia Draven," Mr. Ovalhide said.

"Draven?" Emily's face fell, "is she one of *the* Dravens?"

"Was," Cosmia said, "she's Killian Draven's sister and Myron's aunt. But apparently she's grown apart from her family and appears to want no part in their ways."

"She's also madder than a mad earwig from Madsville," Mr. Ovalhide added, "not that that isn't useful, at times."

"So how can she help us?" I asked.

"She runs a trading post, of sorts, in Coupeville. You'll find it in the hidden, musty room under the feather shop," Cosmia said.

"The what shop?" I asked. I'd never heard of a feather shop before but as I was quickly finding out, on Weirdbey Island, anything was possible.

"Feather shop. They make bedding, duvets and pillows and such forth," Mr. Ovalhide said. "Anyway, you'll find Ophelia in their basement. There's a door at the back and a flight of shifty steps. Take care as you descend. She stores her goods in the basement because she claims it keeps them tamper proof."

"What's she selling?" Jacob asked.

"Mostly manuals and gadgets," Cosmia answered. "Her bailiwick's the supernatural, ESP and psychic defense, that kind of stuff."

"What's psychic self-defense? Is it like karate?" Emily asked.

"Oh, no dear, it's a means of stopping others from leeching away your energy. Emotional vampires, actual vampires, any creature...or person that's attempting to drain your soul dry," Mr. Ovalhide replied.

"Does it actually work?" Emily asked.

"Perhaps," Mr. Ovalhide said, "I'll let you be the judge of that. I subscribe to her newsletter because, well, we like to keep an eye on all things that lean toward the unusual, especially on the island. And this month she's promoting a gadget called a Mind Serpent Squasher. She claims it prevents people from being able to *upload* thoughts into your brain. Whether it works is another matter entirely. But I'd say, under the circumstances, it's worth a shot, and... achoo!"

"She sounds strange," Zach said.

"She doesn't sound any stranger than you," Emily replied.

"True," Jacob added, and smiled.

"Strange or not her wares might be useful in this matter," Mr. Ovalhide said, "and if that fails we'll need to take other measures. Just make sure to use the code *Fubbabaddabooba* and you'll get a thirty percent discount."

"Discount?" Zach asked. "You mean we're about to put ourselves in danger and we're expected to pay for the privilege out of our own pockets?"

"Well," Mr. Ovalhide said, "at this point the Society's funds are as thin as summer ice, what with everyone leaving." He glanced at us carefully. "Do you have any money?"

"Nope," Jacob answered. "We spent the last of it chasing Grimdire and his crew, and we never found a single coin of his treasure or got any reward out of it."

"Give them some money," Cosmia said.

"Indeed," Mr. Ovalhide replied. He got up, opened a pepper pot and unfurled a roll of cash. "I suppose this should go to you now that you've all signed up with us."

"Um, we haven't signed up yet, have we?" I asked. It felt like our misadventure with Captain Grimdire and the Strimples had been a fluke. Plus the pirates were cursed, ghostly and confined to the shadows and gloom whereas Mr. Carrot and his growing army were real. And unlike the pirates, sunlight didn't appear to stop them. There was also the fact that we wouldn't have a giant octopus on our side this time either.

"You'll sign up, believe me," Mr. Ovalhide said, "it's as plain as an overripe onion."

"And a screaming red creeper," Cosmia added. I had no idea what she meant and didn't want to.

"You've got the Society of the Owl and the Wolf written all over you," Mr. Ovalhide added as he rose from the sofa. "Now, scoot off to Coupeville as soon as you can. I'd take you there myself but... achoo!"

"Achoo!" Cosmia added.

"Don't worry, we've got this," Zach said as if he'd been waiting for something like this his whole life. But Emily and Jacob didn't seem quite as convinced.

"Just be sure to report in regularly," Mr. Ovalhide said as he walked us to the door. "Here's my phone number." He handed Zach a business card. "Keep it secure now. That's the Society's secret line. Ah," he opened the door and stood back as we stepped out onto the porch, "daylight. It's still there, safe and sound." And with that he closed the door behind us.

We stopped on the drive and glanced at each other as if none of us could believe what had just happened. It seemed we were part of The Society of the Owl and the Wolf now, whether we wanted to be or not. And with no training, or anything...

I followed the others as they grabbed their bikes and headed to the bus stop, cycling in silence.

. . .

SOON WE WERE SITTING BACK IN OUR SEATS, LOOKING OUT the windows as the bus cruised down the highway. It was empty apart from a lady snoring loudly on the bench by the rear door and a weird man sitting in the very first seat. He was squat and weaselly and had a strange smile that didn't fade as he spoke to the driver. She drummed her hands on the steering wheel and tried to ignore him but I strained to hear what he was saying because he looked like he could easily have been one of Mr. Carrot's followers. All I caught was him asking the driver how her day was, over and over again.

I was about to tell the others when the bus pulled up over to the side of the road. Then my heart seized as I saw the three people getting on.

Eugene King, Cora Crook and Myron Draven.

❦ 14 ❧

LOSERVILLE

Myron Draven's eyes flitted over Zach, then Emily and Jacob. Finally, as they fixed on me a slow, nasty smile spread across his lips. He whispered to Cora and she quickly sat down beside Emily, blocking her in. Then she leaned in toward Zach and mimed biting him. He pulled away, making Myron laugh.

Eugene thundered along the aisle, sat next to Jacob and stared at him like he was a strange new specimen.

Myron locked my gaze as he sat in the seat in front of mine. Finally, he turned to Emily and Zach. "Where are you losers going?" he asked.

"Over to your house in Loserville. Where do you think?" Zach sat up straight but I heard the tremble in his voice. He was terrified. So was I. Fighting wasn't my thing, mostly because I always lost.

"Is that supposed to be funny?" Myron asked.

"It's funnier than anything you could have come up with," Zach said, "and you're about as funny as slipping in dog-"

"Zach!" Emily warned as the bus driver glanced back at us.

Emily gave Myron a withering glare. "There's plenty of room. Maybe you can go and sit somewhere else."

"Yeah, like on another bus in another country," Zach suggested.

"He didn't mean that," Jacob said, as Eugene growled and Cora drummed her fingernails on the rail.

"Yes he did," Myron said. "He thinks he's safe, but he's not. None of you are. We'll see how funny you are once we're back at school." He nodded to Eugene, who shoved himself over on the seat until Jacob was squashed against the window. Then Cora wrapped Emily's hair in her fingers and it seemed like she was about to pull it hard.

"Let them go," I demanded, instantly regretting it.

"And you are?" Myron raised a thick furry eyebrow.

"Dylan." I swallowed, as if trying to gulp my name back down before he heard it.

"Dyyyyylan,' he said, drawing it out until it sounded whiny and ridiculous. "Why'd you cycle away from us yesterday, Dylan? I told you to stop."

"I didn't know what you wanted," I said.

"I wanted to find out why you and your pathetic friends were hassling my uncle."

"Uncle?" I swallowed again. My throat was as dry as old paper. What Uncle? Did he mean Mr. Flittermouse? Or Mr. Ovalhide? Surely...

"What are you dorks doing all the way out here, anyway?" Myron asked. He turned his serpent-like gaze on Zach, as if he was a snake about to strike a mouse. "Investigating pixies? Looking for dragons? You're an idiot, Brillion. You're all idiots and you've got no idea what's coming."

"And you do, I suppose?" Zach asked as he met Myron's stare.

Myron gave a slow nod, but I wasn't convinced he was telling the truth. "Of course."

Then Eugene seemed to get bored because he shoved himself even harder against Jacob, making him squeak under the pressure.

"What's going on back there?" the driver called, ignoring the weirdo at the front who was still jabbering away at her. She gave us a slow, steady glower before glancing at Eugene. "Are you harassing that young man?"

"Nope!" Eugene gazed back defiantly, but he did something I couldn't see to make Jacob cry out again.

With a jerk and a squeal the bus slowed and pulled over by the side of the road. "Out!" The driver pointed.

"Do you know who my father is?" Myron asked.

"Unfortunately, I do," she said with a distasteful look. "Now get off my bus."

"But we're in the middle of nowhere,' Myron protested.

He was right, all I could see was a big field, a few distant houses and nothing much else.

"You should have thought about that before you and your friends started harassing my passengers. It's not the first time we've had this discussion, is it? Now, off."

"But we need to get to Oak Harbor," Cora said as she shot the driver a furious stare.

"Then you have two choices, walk or wait for the next bus," the driver replied.

"That's not for another hour," Myron protested, "this is abuse!"

"Nope, it's an opportunity for you to think about how to behave like civilized people. Now you've got five seconds to get off my bus or I'll radio the next driver and tell him not to stop for you. You want to wander around out here for two hours?" the driver asked.

"Bon voyage, Draven," Zach said. Emily grinned, and Jacob gave a sigh of relief as Eugene slunk off the seat. He stomped past me, mumbling all the way to the exit.

They were almost off the bus when Myron turned and shot a finger toward us. "This isn't over. Not even close."

The rest of our journey was quiet after that, except for the guy chattering at the driver. It was only as we got off the bus that I noticed the stack of flyers in his hand. He *was* one of Carrot's followers.

COUPEVILLE WAS PACKED WITH PEOPLE. THEY MEANDERED down the dark weather-worn boardwalk as the sun broke from the clouds, casting yellow and golden light over the colorful old-fashioned wooden buildings.

I paused, looking out over the calm, shimmering blue cove as it twinkled around the old red building at the end of the pier. It was almost impossible to believe it was the same place the great ghostly pirate galleon had loomed over in the dead of night just a couple of weeks back. Now those same waters looked fun and inviting, and they were peppered with jaunty sail boats and bright colored kayaks. It was almost like none of the bad things could have happened; that there'd been no pirates, ships, or Strimples. Or the gigantic octopus... I shivered as I thought of the wreckage of Captain Grimdire's ship, The Rotten Blight. Was it still lurking beneath that beautiful twinkling water?

Zach and Jacob wound their way through a throng of tourists munching ice cream cones. I ran to catch up as the smell of hot dogs and kettle corn drifted lazily on the breeze.

The feather shop was about halfway down Front Street. It was a small place across from the book store, and its windows were covered in feathers that spelled: 'The Feathered

Nest'. Inside were piles of pillows and mounds of cushions as far back into the shop as I could see. Behind the counter sat a lady with arms so billowy and thick it seemed like they could be stuffed with feathers themselves. She glanced up as we stepped cautiously inside. "I'm guessing you're not here to buy feathers?" she asked.

We shook our heads.

She nodded to the door in the back and the customers browsing through the pillows watched us like we were aliens as we walked toward it. The old wooden door was swollen and jammed. I had to give it a few shoves to get it open. On the other side, on the wall at the top of the stairway, was a huge flyblown poster of a cartoon person's head with bolts of lightning zigzagging toward it and a massive red X crossing it out.

"After you," Emily nodded toward the steps. I was about to start down when she shoved Zach and he stumbled past me, muttering *idiot* as he went.

Jacob swallowed as he glanced after Zach.

"Are you okay?" Emily asked.

"Of course," he said.

I waited until he'd started down the steps before shrugging at Emily.

"Claustrophobia," she whispered, "he doesn't like confined spaces. He gets panic attacks."

"Oh," I said as I followed him, hoping he'd be okay.

The basement was cool and dark. Shelves crammed with books and gadgets lined the walls, as well as things that looked like bizarre musical instruments. Before I could take a closer look a woman leaped out from behind a shelf and regarded us closely.

She was small and wiry and, as she looked us up and down, her stringy purple hair shot around her head. "Ophelia

79

Draven," she said, her voice cracking slightly, "can I help you?" She was soft spoken, but it felt like she was either about to scream or whisper and hadn't decided which.

No one said anything until Jacob finally stepped forward. "Yeah, we're-" he began.

"No!" She held up a finger, and I noticed she was wearing black leather gloves. She traced it in the air before us. "You're emitting a cosmic inkling. And it's very distinct. I'm reading it as..." her face fell, "Oh dear. You're in danger. All of you. Danger!" Her cry echoed around the room.

A heavy, awkward silence fell.

"Right," Emily said, "we're hoping-"

"No!" Ophelia said. "Never rely on hoping. Hope isn't enough in these dark times, dear. You need *knowing*. Unearth, dig, pursue!" She turned to me as she continued. *"Know,* so that they can't get into your mind. *Know,* so they can't spin you around and around and around until you don't know who you are anymore."

"Right," Zach said, "that's why we came, we-"

Ophelia held up her hand again. "I know why you're here. You flee the voice. You've heard it speak. I did too, which is why I left. It's danger. Danger!" Slowly she turned toward me again. I felt a strange lump in the pit of my stomach. The walls seemed to press in and for a moment it felt like it was just me and her as I saw my reflection in her wide piercing green eyes.

"You," she said, "worry me the most. I see darkness around you. Long, twisting paths of night. You'll be the last to go."

"Last to go where?" I asked, my voice stammering.

Her hair whirled through the air as she nodded like she hadn't heard me. "And when you go, there'll be a new age of horror. Horror like you cannot imagine!"

❧ 15 ❧

OPHELIA

The lights flickered and went off, plunging the basement into darkness. Jacob whispered beside me and I heard him draw a long deep breath.

When the lights came back on, Ophelia Draven and I were face to face. I stumbled back, my heart pounding.

"There it goes again," she said, her voice sing-song. "That's the fourth time the power's gone out today. I've already lost track of how many times that's happened this week." A quiet, defiant smile tugged her lips. "Oh, they'd like to keep us in the dark. And do you know why? Because sunlight's the best disinfectant, just like truth!"

"What did you mean when you said I'd be the last to go?" I asked. Her cryptic prophecy of my impending doom was still eating away at me.

She sighed and glanced at each of us in turn. "I'm sorry, I wasn't trying to alarm you, I just call them as I see them. I possess the gift of sight you know. I see things others don't. Sometimes I can see the future in a clump of tea leaves, other times it calls out to me from a splodge of bird droppings. Wherever such signs appear, I can read them as surely as other people read books." I flinched as she placed what she probably thought was a calming hand upon my shoulder.

"At one time," she continued, "my gift made me rich. That was back when I used it for ill, but I've had enough of that life. Now those dark deeds are in my brother's hands alone, and on his conscience."

"Do you mean Killian Draven?" Zach asked.

"Of course," Ophelia said. "He wants nothing less than the world. Right in his palm. He believes everything in creation belongs to him, and his son Myron's no better. They're cut from the same cloth."

"We just ran into Myron on the-" Jacob bit his lips as if stopping himself from saying anything further. He still looked worried as he peered around. I almost suggested he go back upstairs, but I didn't want to embarrass him.

"I hoped Myron would be different," Ophelia said, "I tried to tell him that change is possible. *I* changed, and if I can, anyone can. It happened for me when my brother showed me that... whatever it was..." her eyes clouded, "that thing..."

"What thing?" I asked but she stopped speaking and stared at the wall.

Finally, she looked back at me, as if she'd only just heard my question. "I don't remember. Even though I'm certain I managed to resist it. I've always been willful, you see. But how it tried to pull the wool over my eyes! Still, I wouldn't let it. You've got to know yourself. Know your flaws and shortcomings. If you know yourself, then they can't control you."

"They?" Emily asked.

"They. It's always they," Ophelia said, "they're too cowardly to be a singular."

"That's kind of why we're here. We need to stop someone who was trying to mess with our minds," Zach said.

Ophelia's face fell as we explained what had happened at the tent. "Classic mind control techniques," she said. "You can't let them in!"

"How do we stop it from happening again?" Jacob asked.

"Well," Ophelia's face lit up again, "the first step's to get away from the controllers. That's what I did; I cut myself off from the hooligans and set up my little underground shop, pardon the pun. Now I dedicate my days to helping others guard themselves against the insidious grips of ne'er do wells. Having a purpose, goals and convictions of your own definitely helps prevent attempts at mind control."

"Do you have anything, like a tool or a machine to stop the voice from getting into our heads?" I asked.

"Yeah, we need to go back to the tent and figure out where the voice came from so we can stop it," Zach added.

"Well, as I said, the best solution is to keep away from this ghastly tent." Ophelia sighed. "Mind control relies on the perpetrator being as near to their targets as possible. Be it a person, phone, or a television program. Program, get it?" She cackled madly, and then seemed to remember herself. "Do you have any suspects or suspicions as to who this ghastly culprit might be?"

"We think it might be a man called Jepa Cloak," Jacob replied.

"That name..." her eyes dimmed, "I know it... But why? It's so familiar." She shook her head. "No, it's gone. Wiped from my memory like a greasy smudge from a window. But why approach this Mr. Cloak if you believe he's dangerous? Why not stay away?"

"Because we can't." Zach puffed his chest out as he added, "we're on a mission for a secret society. I can't give their name or details, but let's just say they're an ancient, powerful organization."

Emily sighed. "We need to find the missing people, and we think Jepa Cloak's behind it. It all seemed to start when he arrived. But we can't get near him because of the voice. Plus, he's got followers everywhere, not to mention his creepy assistant, Mr. Carrot."

"And that dude's as mad as a mad earwig from..." Zach's words tailed off as Ophelia glanced toward him.

"Where on the island did this occur?" she asked. She looked terrified, as if her biggest fears were coming real. The lights flickered again and heavy footsteps stomped across the ceiling. Her face turned even paler as she grasped my sleeve. "Where?"

❧ 16 ❧

THE MIND SERPENT SQUASHER

I waited for the lights to flicker back on and the thumping footsteps to fade away before answering Ophelia. "Most of the disappearances seem to be going on in and around Langley, but it could be happening in other places too."

Ophelia shook her head. "Perhaps it's time for a vacation."

"You're leaving?" Zach asked. "What is it with adults on this island?"

She grasped his wrist. "I can't let them get to me, not again! I can't risk it, I must remain untethered so I can spread my message to the world. Don't you see?"

"All I see is you running away. Just like everyone else does," Zach replied.

Ophelia sighed. "Maybe you're right. I'm sorry, really I am. But I've already had one brush with the darkness, I can't face another. Now," her voice hardened, "I've warned you to stay away from this dastardly force, but you seem determined to place yourselves in its path-"

"We're not going to run away from this. We're not cowards. People have gone missing and we have to find them," I said. Such blunt statements were usually Zach's department, but I was starting to feel angry too. He was right. The last time things had gone wrong with Captain Grimdire everyone else had run away, and now it was happening again.

"Well," Ophelia said, "if you intend to face this beast you'll need protection."

"Mr. Oval..." Zach began, then stopped. "Our employer, who for obvious reasons cannot be named, told us you sold something called a Mind Serpent Squasher."

"And that there's a discount too," Jacob added, "if we use the code..." he glanced at his phone, "Fubbabaddabooba!"

"The name of my very first pet squirrel," Ophelia smiled, but a moment later it faded. "I'm afraid we had a rush of orders on the serpent squasher recently. There's only one left in the shop, but it's for my own personal use only. Still, I suppose I could lend it to you while I'm gone." She gave us a long earnest look and vanished behind the counter.

When she reappeared, she held up something that looked like a huge glimmering tiara. Glowing pink crystals capped the ends of bands that were wrapped in what looked like foil. She placed it on her head and flicked a switch on the side. The tiara hummed loudly, and the crystals shone even brighter as they lit up the foil with a soft pink glow.

A heavy droning buzz filled the basement, as if a gigantic bee was trapped in the walls. When Ophelia spoke, she had to shout. "The first step to using the Mind Serpent Squasher is to block out all thoughts but your own. To know who you are!" She steadied the tiara with her hands as she stepped carefully toward us. "Then," she tapped a long fingernail on the crystals, "these little beauties help neutralize any bad intentions that might be attempting to snake their way in. And tucked away under this foil are the silver prongs that prevent psychic interference. Silver, as you probably know-"

"Repels vampires," Zach finished, nodding his head.

"Exactly!" Ophelia looked pleased with him.

Emily said something but I couldn't hear her over the droning din.

Ophelia flicked the switch and slowly it began to fade. "Sorry, dear, I didn't catch that. What did you say?"

"I asked if you have anything smaller. Or quieter."

"Our mission requires stealth," Zach agreed. "Basically, we need to slip inside the tent, take out the bad guy, and be gone before they even know we were there."

"Hmmm. Then maybe the Mind Serpent Squasher isn't the right tool for the job." Carefully, Ophelia removed it from her head and set it down. "I have other things you can use for more general protection. They'll certainly help, but first and foremost, get yourselves prepared because it's only you who can help yourselves. Remember, these con artists always start by telling you what they think you want to hear, and any aversion to the truth is their back door into your mind."

We followed her as she marched over to a shelf and picked out four pendants. The silvery-gray polished stone drops on the chains shone below the lights. "Hematite," she said. "It's a protective stone. See, it looks like armor because it is armor. And the chains are pure silver of course-"

"For warding off those vampires you mentioned," Jacob said. He sounded doubtful. I felt the same.

"How much are they?" Emily asked, as she took out the money Mr. Ovalhide had given us.

Ophelia shook her head. "Nope, your money's no good here, not today. These are on the house. And..." she looked up as the lights flickered again, "I'll wish you luck. The best of luck. You'll need it."

Her eyes flitted to me and it seemed she had more to say, but didn't. It made me feel even worse. I wanted to get back into daylight fast. For my sake as much as Jacob's.

"Thanks," Emily said, and the rest of us thanked her too, even though I wasn't sure the pendants would help when it came down to it. We hadn't even met Jepa Cloak yet, but we knew his army of followers were bad news and they were growing by the day.

Then, as we left, Jacob paused to look at the bulletin board on the wall by the stairwell. It was covered with notes, clippings and pictures. One was of Ophelia sitting in the middle of a circle of squirrels dressed like toy soldiers. Another was a newspaper article announcing the opening of her store. Next to that was an image of her on a windy bluff by the sea, and beside her stood... Mr. Carrot, mad wiry mustard hair and all!

"Wait," Jacob said, "you know Mr. Carrot?"

"Mr. Carrot?" She wandered over, glanced at the image and gave a high, fast laugh. "That's my brother."

"I thought you said Killian Draven's your brother?" Emily said.

"He is," Ophelia replied. "I have *two* brothers. One is light, the other is total darkness."

"Which one's the light?" Zach asked, not even bothering to hide his sarcasm.

"Ambrose. Poor, poor Ambrose."

"But he's Mr.-" Zach begun until Ophelia cut him off.

"A good man," she said, her voice defensive, "and a most misunderstood one too. He'd have taken mankind to the furthest reaches of the galaxy by now if it hadn't had been for the *incident*. Not that it was his fault, well not entirely."

"Incident?" I asked.

The sides of Ophelia's face flushed. "He... there was an explosion." She thrust her hands before her. "No one died! No one was harmed, which was a miracle in itself. Although, I suppose when all's said and done it did destroy an entire laboratory. That much is indisputable. Naturally NASA got all upset about it, and that was the end of his career."

"What was he researching when it happened?" Jacob asked.

"He never said, and neither did the authorities. The whole thing was hushed up. I think..." a dark look crossed her face again, "I think someone got to him."

"Who?" Emily asked.

"Killian, our older brother. He always tries to control everything!"

I glanced at the others. No one seemed to want to tell her what we suspected *Mr. Carrot* had been up to. "Have you seen him recently?" I asked, hoping she would tell us something useful.

"No, not for weeks now. He's stopped talking to me, it seems. I assume Killian put him up to it. They don't want me to know what they're up to, probably because they know I won't approve."

"Where does Ambrose live?" Zach asked.

I gave him a long stern stare, thinking he'd probably suggest we go there next to get a closer look at him.

"I've no idea," Ophelia said, much to my relief. "He had to sell his old place after he lost his job and since then we became estranged."

I wasn't sure what estranged meant exactly, but she was definitely strange and so was Mr. Carrot. I watched as Jacob glanced to the stairs. He wasn't looking well. "Well, thanks again for the stones," I said. It was time to go.

She paused to grip my shoulder. "Don't let him in. Hold firm!"

"I don't understand," I said.

"You will. And I wish it wasn't so."

. . .

No one spoke as we caught the bus, but I saw the others glancing at their pendants. Would they really protect us when it came to it? I doubted it.

And then, as I glanced at the driver, who was the same lady who'd driven us to Coupeville, I saw her eyes in the mirror. She was staring ahead, blankly, almost robotically. And then her nose twitched just like a rabbit's. She'd been turned.

Soon it would be everyone on the whole island.

17

DRINK THE NIGHT

That night the voice from the tent filled my dreams. It purred up from under my bed, its whispers drifting through the air like the sweet scent of syrupy pancakes on a lazy Sunday morning. The wily words slipped into my ears and lodged themselves in my mind. I shook my head to try and force them out, but they wouldn't budge.

"Go," the voice whispered.

"Where?" I asked, my heart racing.

"Out into the trees. You're so, so thirsty, Dylan. Go and drink the night."

I woke to find myself standing at my bedroom door. My fingers trembled as they clutched the cold round handle. I forced myself back into bed, but didn't dare to sleep again until daylight began to seep in around the edges of the curtains.

Had the voice been real, or was it just a dream? It was becoming hard to tell which was which. All I knew was we had to stop Mr. Carrot and Mr. Cloak because, if we didn't, everything would be lost.

. . .

T HAT MORNING M OM ANNOUNCED THAT SHE AND D AD were going over to the mainland, or America as some Weirdbey islanders called it. Then she watched in horror as I put on my sneakers.

"I can't believe you're actually putting those filthy, old shoes on your feet, Dylan. They should be condemned and destroyed in a controlled explosion." She rolled her eyes and looked at my father as she shook her head.

Translation: I was going shopping now too.

I had no idea how things would be over there in the real world, but as we drove off the ferry everything seemed totally normal. People acted like people usually did. They didn't have strange, secretive smiles and their eyes weren't glazed, staring or distant. It was like the rest of the world was just carrying on as it always did, while Weirdbey Island was sinking into madness.

※

I CALLED MY FRIENDS AS SOON AS I GOT BACK HOME. Z ACH and Emily's parents had gone out and left their sister Violet in charge, so we all decided to meet at the park in Langley. I hadn't really talked to Violet since our battle with Captain Grimdire, but the few times she'd seen me, she'd scowled, so I figured she hated me too now.

"Well? Did you find anything yet?" Zach asked, for at least the fifth time as Jacob thumbed through the browser on his phone.

"Stop nagging, Zachary," Emily said, "he's looking."

Suddenly Jacob slapped his forehead. "I've been searching

under the wrong name. I should be searching for Draven, not Carrot!"

I glanced around to make sure no one could hear us but the whole town seemed to be under the eerie, trance-like spell now, so it didn't matter.

"Found him!" Jacob turned the phone so we could see the headline on the local newspaper's website. It read;

'Nuisance Noise Dispute!'

"What noise?" I asked as Jacob flicked through the article.

"Apparently," he said, "Draven and his wife moved into a new house out on Sand Dollar Lane a few months ago…"

"That's pretty close to where the tent is!" Emily said.

"So, what happened?" Zach asked as he strained to read the article over Jacob's shoulder.

"Well," Jacob continued, "soon after the Dravens moved in, the neighbors started complaining about strange noises *in the middle of the night.*"

"Like what?" Zach asked.

"Drilling, thumping. Deep underground booms. And their power kept going out as well. They insisted that it started when Draven and his wife moved in. But then…" Jacob flicked further down the page. "When the journalist returned to follow up on her story, she said the neighbors had changed their minds, that they said they couldn't have been happier with the new arrivals." He glanced up. "He must have used his mind control device on them!"

"We need to look into this," Zach said.

We grabbed our bikes and rode off as the hot July sunshine baked the shimmering pavement.

SAND DOLLAR LANE WASN'T A VERY LONG ROAD AND IT DEAD ended in a wide round cul-de-sac lined with several big white houses. They were huge, stately. Their windows gleamed and the lawns stretching out before them were the deepest green I'd ever seen. Zach pointed out a couple of security cameras, but other than that, no one seemed to be around.

Beyond the houses and their manicured yards we could see the woods that towered over the meadow. It was clammy and hot but I still shivered as I recalled the zombie-like people who'd chased us out of there and the mysterious Jepa Cloak, hiding in his tent like some terrible secret.

"It's this one," Emily called as she checked the mail boxes and pointed to the name 'Draven'. "Woah, Ophelia said they'd downgraded, I can't imagine what their last place looked like!"

It seemed like no one was home, and I was about to take a closer look when Jacob called us over.

"Look," he nodded to the side of the house and as I followed his gaze I caught a glimpse of a large red and green striped tent. It was exactly like the one we'd seen in the woods and parked next to it was a bunch of heavy machinery including a big old yellow digger covered in fresh earth.

We cycled down the path that ran alongside of the house, past a rose garden, and across the lawn and skidded to a stop by the tent's opening. Sounds came from inside; a deep distant drilling that seemed to be shaking the ground below our feet.

"What's in there?" Zach nodded for me to open the flap. I reached for it but froze as a long shadow fell over me.

A voice broke the easy summer's afternoon peace like a crack of thunder. "And just what do you think you're doing?" a woman demanded.

18

DASTARDLY PLANS

The woman behind us was tall and her fancy blonde hair was shaped and styled like a model from a magazine. She wore huge dark beetle-like sunglasses, and a long white summer dress. In her hand was a watering can, and she held it so loosely it was dripping on the grass. "Can I help you?" she asked in an odd calm sort of tone but since I couldn't see her eyes, or read the expression on her face it really unsettled me.

"No. Yes. We..." I stumbled over my words and glanced to the others for help.

"We're looking for our cat," Zach said quickly. He gave a slight shrug like it wasn't any of her business, even though we were standing right in the middle of what I guessed was her yard.

"Cat?" the woman asked as she glanced around the garden. "Do you live in this neighborhood? I haven't seen you before."

"Well I haven't seen you before either," Zach replied. "The name's Zach. And you are?"

"Millicent Draven. And you didn't answer my question, do you live around here?"

"No," Emily said, "we're from Langley."

"Are you?" Mrs. Draven gazed at us for another quiet moment before continuing. "Then this is an awfully long way for your cat to have wandered, no?"

"Actually," Zach said, "we were taking her for a walk. She's got a health condition and we have to walk her at least five miles a day."

"Does she ride a bicycle too?" Mrs. Draven asked as she nodded to where our bikes laid sprawled across the lawn.

"She runs alongside us," Zach said, "she's really fast."

"She must be." Mrs. Draven nodded to the house. "You'd better come inside."

"No, we need-" Emily began.

"Please." Mrs. Draven's voice was more forceful now. "Come in while I call the neighbors." She gave us a lopsided smile. "We'll find your cat in no time. What's her name?"

"Um," Zach glanced to the sky and I could tell he was struggling to come up with a name. I cringed as I waited to hear what he was going to say. "Cat!" he blurted out.

"Your cat's called Cat?" Mrs. Draven raised a plucked eyebrow over her sunglasses.

"No," Zach said, "yes! Yes, it's short for... Cattywhumpus."

"Right, well come on, let's find Cattywhumpus together. Then you can be on your way." Mrs. Draven led us to the house. It felt like we had no choice but to follow her.

"Keep your eyes peeled," Zach whispered.

The place was nice and cool. It was filled with white space and high ceilings, and the kitchen seemed larger than our entire house. It was also perfectly tidy, apart from a crate full of carrots on the counter, and a jug of bright juice that matched the orange glass light fixtures hanging down from the kitchen ceiling.

"Would you like a drink?" Mrs. Draven asked.

"Yes. No," Zach said. He shook his head as if he was warning us, like we needed to be told something was seriously wrong here. "Thanks though."

"Are you speaking for everyone?" Mrs. Draven asked as she regarded the rest of us. We nodded dumbly. She snatched her sunglasses off. Her eyes were glazed and dim, just like the rest of Ambrose Draven's followers. They'd gotten to her too...

Mrs. Draven stumbled around the room as if searching for something. "I can't for the life of me remember what I did with my phone." She glanced back at us. "I haven't been using it much these days, which is probably why I can't remember where it is," she explained, "but I'll find it soon enough and we'll have you reunited with Cattywhumpus in no time. Now wait here." She strode from the kitchen down a long corridor, her footsteps silenced by the thick plush carpet.

"We need to take a good look around while we can," Zach kept his voice low as he gave Emily a pointed look.

"I'm not going anywhere," she said. "She gives me the creeps!"

"The coin if you will," Zach said to Jacob.

"The coin it is," Jacob said. He took it from his pocket and called tails. We called after him and for some stupid reason I said heads.

A cold, sick feeling passed through my stomach and Jacob looked at me like I was a man condemned. "It's on you, Dylan," he said.

Yeah, I knew that.

"Check as many rooms as you can, get the lay of the land and find out if there's a basement," Zach said, "they've got to be hiding those missing people somewhere."

"What if she catches me?" I asked.

"Pretend you're looking for the bathroom," Emily suggested.

"Right." Slowly, hesitantly, I walked across the kitchen, down the plush carpet, and past the long white walls. There was no sign of Mrs. Draven and I wished I'd paid more attention to where she'd gone.

The place was silent and still. If any of the others had dropped a pin on the kitchen floor, I'd probably have heard it. Which meant I should have been able to hear if anyone was stashed away in the house. Unless the walls were soundproofed... I gulped as I imagined a room of people chained up, their mouths gagged, their eyes stricken with terror. Was that what was going to happen to us?

I was nearing the end of the hall and I still couldn't see Mrs. Draven. I glanced back. The kitchen seemed at least a mile away.

Then I spotted the door beside me. I tried the handle. It opened...

The room inside was the total opposite of the rest of the house. It was crammed full of stuff, and there was clutter everywhere. Dirty clothes, plates of half eaten toast, and notebooks filled with messy black writing. I saw several odd gadgets; weird looking tools, gleaming golden screwdrivers and piles of nuts and bolts scattered upon the desk in the corner.

It had to be Ambrose Draven's work room. Or Mr. Carrot, as he was now called.

My gaze fell to the cork board at the end of the room. It was so big it covered almost the entire wall. Sheets of paper with weird sketches were pinned across the center of it. They looked like drawings of... lots and lots of... dark tubes. No not tubes, what were they?

As I looked again, I saw the collage made one huge picture, and what I'd mistaken for tubes formed a maze of tunnels... My thoughts jumped back to the heavy machinery we'd seen outside the tent. Was that what the neighbors had been hearing at night? Draven digging? And if so, what was he digging for?

On one side of the cork board were diagrams and blueprints for weird, cone-shaped devices. The lines he'd scrawled around them looked like sound waves. I took photos of them with my phone.

Spread across the desk was a map of the world and a huge red X was crossed through a tiny speck of land. It took a moment to realize it was Whidbey Island. Beyond it, thousands of tiny green arrows pointed to the rest of the world. I got pictures of that too.

I was about to rifle through a pile of papers to see if there was anything else of interest when someone spoke. I jumped so high I thought I'd hit the ceiling.

The voice was coming from outside the room, and it was getting louder.

I scurried to the door and slipped through. I was about to run back to the kitchen when a shadow fell across the carpet from a room down the hall. Whoever was speaking was in there.

Was it Mrs. Draven? No, it was a man's voice. Mr. Draven? I gulped as I tip-toed toward it and glanced around the edge of the doorframe.

Mrs. Draven was standing inside, facing a wall. She gestured to it with her hands as if she was speaking to it. "They know," she said.

Who was she talking to? Had she gone completely insane? Were we stuck in a house with a crazy woman?

We had to get out, fast! I was about to sprint down the hall when her voice shifted, and suddenly, it sounded like a man's voice. The same man who'd whispered in my mind...

"We saw them arrive," he said, "we watched as they tried to

peek inside the tent. They *mustn't* go in there, they mustn't know. Not yet. Not until it's too late for them."

Mrs. Draven shifted her head. When she spoke again, it was in her own voice. "What do you want me to do?"

She shifted again as the man answered. "Keep them there. Stall them. The others are on their way. They'll deal with them. Those little fools won't know what's hit them."

19

FOUND OUT

My heart pounded so hard I was sure Mrs. Draven would hear it. I strode down the corridor as fast as I could, forcing myself not to break into a full-on run. I didn't want her to know I was there. I had to warn the others before she got back. We had to get out, fast.

A door creaked behind me. I slowed and took a deep breath as I glanced back.

"Did you find what you were looking for?" Mrs. Draven asked, her smile empty. Her eyes were dimmer than ever as they gazed at me. She looked like a strange, glassy eyed doll.

"I... I was just looking for the bathroom." I hadn't needed it before but it was starting to feel like I would soon.

"It doesn't appear you found it. You look uncomfortable. Don't be, everything's fine. Actually, it's better than fine. Come with me, I'll show you where it is."

"I... I don't need it now. Thanks anyway. We've got to get going."

"No." Her smile was plastic and fake. "Oh, no! You can't go yet." She stepped toward me. I stood my ground, unwilling to turn my back on her.

"Why?" I asked, trying to keep my tone light, like there was no problem.

"Because we haven't found your kitty cat yet, have we?" She slipped a hand into the pocket of her dress and pulled out a sleek silver phone. "Let me call the neighbors. You and your friends can wait and sample my delicious carrot juice."

I didn't want any of her *delicious carrot juice*. I wanted to grab the others and get out of there. But fear held me rooted to the spot. It took everything I had to force myself to back away down the corridor.

"You and your friends can wait and sample my delicious carrot juice," she said again, like a broken robot. "You and your friends can wait and sample my delicious carrot juice." She strode faster toward me.

I sprinted down the hall. My legs felt like they were made of jelly as I stumbled into the kitchen.

The others glanced at me, looking worried. I shook my head slightly, and opened my eyes wide to warn them. "What's that?" I asked loudly, "oh you found her? Great!"

"Found who?" Zach asked as Mrs. Draven appeared behind me.

"The cat," Jacob said quickly, "yes, we found Cattywhumpus." He nodded to me and I nodded back.

"Cool," I said, almost shouting, "well we should probably head home then." I tried not to flinch as Mrs. Draven stepped into the kitchen, her eyes staring emptily. She strode past me and stood in front of the patio doors. "You can't leave," she said. "Not yet."

"We've got to," I said. I reached for the doors but she blocked me. I tried to go the other way, but she leaped in front of me like we were playing some kind of silly game.

Mrs. Draven held her phone up, and I heard the snapping sound effect of a shutter as she photographed us. "You and your friends can wait and sample my delicious carrot juice." She said, again and again.

"Oh no!" Emily said.

I followed her gaze to the street outside. Mr. Draven's van was pulling up. He jumped out along with three of his followers and they strode toward the house.

We had to get to our bikes, and fast.

I lunged for the doors again but Mrs. Draven shrieked madly as she blocked me. "Everything's gone cattywhumpus!" she cried and began laughing, hollering and screeching like a demon.

❧ 20 ❧

CONEY ISLAND WAY

I was desperate to get outside, but Mrs. Draven was standing right in front of the doors.

Her husband and his followers would arrive at any moment. I glanced around for somewhere to hide. The rooms were so sparse and orderly. There was no cover. But as I looked again an idea flashed through my mind.

I sprang for the box of carrots.

"Don't touch my little orange treasures!" Mrs. Draven cried as I seized the box. Panic flashed in her eyes as she bounded toward me, and away from the patio doors. I heaved the box into the air and the carrots rained down upon the carpet.

Mrs. Draven screamed and sank to her knees as she scooped them up. "These are the best ones, bless their tiny carrot hearts! They're too precious for juicing!" She spoke to them like they were her babies. "Oh, my poor little scrumpkins!"

We swarmed toward the patio. As I wrenched the handles; the front door burst open and Ambrose Draven appeared. His usually pale face was crimson with anger, and his mustard colored hair stuck up higher than ever. "Stop!" he cried.

His followers barged past him and raced toward us.

"Run!" I shouted, as if anyone needed telling. We sped across the lawn toward the pile of bikes by the tent. I was about to grab mine when a breeze made the flap ripple. I pulled the canvas back and stole a glance inside.

A huge hole, one large enough to swallow up a school bus, had been torn from the grass and it plummeted deep down into the earth. Strings of golden-yellow lights marked its walls, and twinkled off into the cavernous shadows. The hole was unlike anything I'd ever seen before.

"Dylan!" Emily called.

I spun around to find the others cycling away, and Emily gesturing for me to follow.

Ambrose Draven was nearly on me, and so were his followers. My fingers trembled as I grabbed my handlebars and wrenched my bike up from the ground. I jumped on the seat and kicked down on the pedals as Draven's shadow fell over me. "You'll pay for your insolence boy. Oh how you'll pay!"

My bike lurched as he leaped toward me. I raced away, wobbling madly as his followers lunged for me.

"Boyyyyyyy!" The voice came from the tent. *"Stopppppppp!"*

It got right into my mind. I could only watch as my fingers reached for the brakes, it was like they belonged to someone else.

Everything seemed to go into slow motion.

"No!" I forced myself to grab the necklace. My fingers brushed the stone and its warmth jogged me from the trance. "Don't listen!" I shouted to myself as I fought to block the whispers from entering my mind.

Shadows loomed across the lawn.

They were gaining on me.

I cycled harder, my bike pitching as I threw everything I had into it.

Then, as the voice came again, I pinched the back of my hand to try and break its spell. Free of its hypnotic grasp, I cycled past the side of the house and out onto the street where the others waited. They took off as soon as they saw I was on my way and we all cycled as fast as we could.

An engine rumbled behind us. I glanced back to see Draven's followers jumping into his van. I felt his gaze lock onto mine. "They're coming!" I shouted. The others peered back.

"Get off the road!" Emily called.

We shot off the asphalt toward the meadow stretching between us and the woods. My wheels juddered over the ground and the high grass whipped my ankles. The van's roaring engine grew louder as we raced for the trees.

Screeeeee

I glanced back to see Draven's van skidding to a stop at the side of the road. Then he and his goons piled out and watched from the verge. One of the followers started to stumble after us but Draven called him back.

We'd escaped, but the clock was ticking. Draven's wife had pictures of us now. It wouldn't take long for them to find out who we were and where we lived.

LANGLEY WAS JAM PACKED AS WE CYCLED DOWN THE HILL and headed for the park. It was on the outskirts of the hustle and bustle that attracted the tourists, so it was quiet there, as usual. We sat down at the picnic table under the old awnings and caught our breath.

"What are we going to do now?" I asked. It was starting to feel like there was nothing we could do, but I kept the thought to myself.

"I need a drink," Zach said.

I nodded. "My throat's as dry as sandpaper." It had gotten really humid, like a storm was about to break and the thick gray clouds had trapped all the summer heat in. Once we'd got our bearings straight we cycled to the store to get some drinks.

The others went inside while I watched the bikes and kept a look out for Ambrose Draven. Then my gaze fell on the headlines of the local newspaper in the window of the news stand. They all seemed to say exactly the same thing, only in different words:

"One night left before The Extraordinary Celebration!"

'Langley prepares for a most amazing transformation!'

'Big changes come to Whidbey Island!'

There was a picture of a rabbit silhouetted against a full moon and below it were details of the event. It was starting at 8 pm tomorrow night, in the middle of town. Another headline read:

'Langley streets to be renamed!'

Apparently First Street was now Hare Street, Second Street was 'Coney Island Way' and Anthes Avenue had become Bunny Lane. It felt like Jepa Cloak, or whoever he really was, had already won.

"What's wrong?" Emily asked as she tossed a cold bottle of water to me.

I nodded to the newspapers. "Maybe we're too late. They're not even trying to hide it now."

"It's never too late," Zach said. Usually he was the first to fold, but it seemed like he was still reveling in his new position. "We're the Society of the Owl and the Wolf. We've got to fight with everything we have."

Jacob looked worried as he scanned the headlines, but then he fixed his glasses on his nose. "Yeah, we can't let Cloak win."

"We don't even know who or what Cloak is," I said.

"Then we need to find out," Emily said.

I nodded. They were right, we couldn't give up. We'd beaten Captain Grimdire and his pirates and that had seemed like something impossible at the time. I took a long swallow of cold water. "We've still got our pendants," I said, even though they didn't seem like much more than wishful trinkets.

"Exactly." Zach held his up so it gleamed in the sunlight. "Mind serpents away!"

"Dylan!"

I glanced toward the store and saw my mom cradling a bag of groceries. "Hey, Mom."

She gave me a curious look, like she knew something was troubling me. Then she appraised the others and smiled. She'd met Emily already but not Jacob or Zach. Once she'd introduced herself she turned back to me. "I was about to message you. We're eating early tonight."

"How come?" I asked.

"Your father and I have a date," she smiled and the sides of her face flushed. "Come on, I'll give you a ride home."

"Sure," I said. It was probably best for us to be off the streets anyway.

"We'll meet up tomorrow," Zach said, eyeing my mom cautiously, "and figure out a new plan of attack."

"For what?" Mom asked.

"Just a pest control issue," Zach said.

Mom raised an eyebrow but then she spotted a garage sale flyer on the store's bulletin board and started noting down the details while the others said goodbye and rode off.

When she'd finished, I followed her across the lot, lifted my bike into the trunk of her car and we drove through the town. Along the way I spotted several new clusters of hypnotized followers lingering on the sidewalks, I was glad for the cover the car provided, glad they couldn't see me with their, dull, listless eyes.

"GREAT!" JAMIE GROWLED. I LOOKED UP FROM MY BOOK AS he cursed at his stupid game. I hated having to listen to it, but at least it kept him busy while Mom and Dad were out. Then the television flickered again, the lights flickered, everything seemed to flicker.

I wanted to tell him how there were worse things than power outages, but I didn't. Let him enjoy his time, I thought. *The extraordinary celebration* was nearly upon us and all I knew was that it felt like it was probably going to be the total opposite of whatever might inspire a celebration. Bad things were coming, and as much as I disliked Jamie, I didn't want to see anyone harmed. Not even him.

Wilson plonked his nose on my knee. A faded red rubber ring pitted with teeth marks hung from his slobbery jaw. He dropped it onto my lap.

I held it out to him and he took it carefully. Then he pulled one way and I pulled the other. It was one of his favorite games.

As Wilson pulled, his teeth gritted with determination, and I realized Emily and the others were right. We couldn't give up. We knew what was going on, but everyone else - Jamie, my parents, and the whole town - didn't have a clue. That meant we had a responsibility to fight back, with everything we had.

I pretended to lose my grip on the ring and watched Wilson parade around the carpet with his prize. Then he returned, wiggling his tail in victory and gazing at me as he waited for me to grab it. But I knew he'd pull away as soon as I tried.

"Give me it!" I gave a fake growl and lunged for the toy.

Wilson jumped back, his tail sweeping the air. It was a nice, normal moment in what had been one of the craziest days I'd ever had.

Then we both looked up as a key rattled in the lock. Mom and Dad strode in, looking really pleased with themselves.

"Hey!" Mom said. She looked strange. Distracted. Like she wasn't fully there.

"Hi." I forced a smile as I glanced at Dad. He had the same dreamy look as Mom. "Where'd you go?" I asked. My stomach felt like it was plummeting. I already knew what was coming.

"To see a fortune teller. The amazing Jepa Cloak!" Dad said.

"That's dumb," Jamie called as he gunned down a line of glowing aliens.

"No, it really wasn't." Mom eyes were almost as wide as her smile. "You wouldn't believe what he told us."

"No, I wouldn't," I said under my breath so only Wilson could hear me.

"Yeah, I'd usually consider myself a major skeptic when it comes to hocus-pocus like that," Mom said, "but this was something else."

"Really!" Dad agreed and his whole face wrinkled with his grin. "But you can see for yourselves," he added.

"What do you mean?" I fought to control the tremble in my voice.

"All will be revealed," Mom said, with a cheesy wink.

"Tomorrow," Dad added, "at the extraordinary celebration. We've got tickets. We're all going!"

THE EXTRAORDINARY
CELEBRATION TIMES

"When?" Emily's voice was so loud that the squirrel watching us outside the window of the tree house, bolted away.

My nerves were rattled. I'd hardly slept knowing the extraordinary celebration was coming tonight. The others were the same. It turned out all of our parents had bought tickets, which meant we had to go, one way or another.

"This morning," Jacob said.

"This morning what?" I asked. I'd missed at least half of what she'd said.

"Ophelia Draven went missing." Emily sounded exasperated and not just because I'd failed to keep up with the conversation. "She was supposed to open her store this morning and never showed up. The lady who runs the feather shop stopped by her apartment to check on her and said she wasn't there, and her front door was wide open. She's gone, and the news people are trying to make out it's because she's mad."

"Well she *is* mad," Zach said.

"And so are you," Emily folded her arms, "but I'm not going to let them take you away, am I?"

"We've got to help her," I said, "she helped us. Or tried to."

"We've got to help *everyone,*" Zach said, as he fiddled with the necklace Ophelia Draven had given us. "Do you think this thing is actually going to work? I mean it's just a little hunk of stone, right?"

"I hope they work," I said. But I felt just as doubtful as Zach sounded.

"I guess we'll soon find out," Jacob said.

"I can't believe we're going back there," I muttered.

"We don't have much choice," Jacob replied, "we've got to find out what's in the tent and how they're broadcasting Jepa Cloak's voice into people's minds. If we can disrupt it, then maybe we can wake people up." He checked his watch. "We've got eleven hours until the extraordinary celebration begins."

"But they've already seen us, and Mrs. Draven has got pictures of us" I said. "They know what we look like. As soon as we get near the tent, they'll grab us."

"Then they can't see us coming." Emily gave me a mischievous look and her eyes twinkled.

"Have you got some kind of invisibility cloak you haven't told me about?" Zach asked. "It'd explain a lot."

"Nope," Emily said, "but there's a thrift store in town."

Jacob nodded slowly. "Disguises..."

"I'm not wearing some old man's Long Johns again. Or moss," Zach said. I grinned as I remembered how we'd dressed him up when we'd gone up against the Strimples. "I'm not doing it," Zach jabbed his finger into the air, "and I don't care what the coin of doom says!"

"Don't freak out," Emily said, "we're just going to get some different clothes from the thrift store, stuff they won't recognize us in. Plus I've still got props and make-up from the play."

"Play?" I asked.

"She does stupid school plays," Zach said, "they're soooo boring."

"Shut up, Zachary, they're not stupid" Emily said, "you are. I suppose you think you've got a better idea."

"Maybe I do!" Zach grinned fiercely, but slowly his smile faded.

"Well?" Emily asked as she tapped her foot on the boards.

"Maybe I don't," Zach said, his voice small and quiet.

"Right." Emily headed for the ladder. "Let's go then."

IT WAS ALREADY GETTING HOT AS WE CYCLED DOWN THE hill into town. I fell behind as I glanced into the yards, and found many of them filled with tiny rabbits leaping across their lawns. Where were they coming from? They seemed to have started appearing around the same time Jepa Cloak had. Was it a coincidence? I was about to ask the others when I saw how far ahead they were and cycled fast to catch them up.

The thrift shop was a large building on the corner across from the park. Mannequins and creepy old toys lined the windows, the kind that felt like they'd spring to life if you turned your back on them. Zach was about to push the door open when a mean, drawling voice came from behind us, freezing us in our tracks. "I always figured that's where you guys got your clothes."

It was Eugene, Myron Draven's right-hand thug. He sneered as he held his phone up and snapped pictures of us.

"So what if we do get our clothes here?" Emily asked, posing a smile for his camera.

Eugene lowered the phone. His brow furrowed and it seemed like he was looking really hard for a smart reply.

"Keep working on it," Emily said, "it'll come to you at some point this century."

Eugene growled and began to lurch toward Emily, but he paused as he glanced at the rest of us.

"Bingo! That's right," Zach said, "four against one. I don't fancy your chances, punk." He stood tall until his wild hair was almost level with Eugene's wobbling chin. "And don't ever growl at my sister again."

"We'll crush you losers," Eugene said.

"No doubt," Jacob agreed, "but not today."

We watched as Eugene stomped away, his phone clamped to the side of his reddening face.

"We've probably got about ten minutes until Myron and Cora get here," Emily said, "so we need to get this done fast."

I followed her into the thrift store, which was already packed with shoppers, and Emily led us to the clothes racks. I was glad one of us had a plan.

WE LEFT WITH BAGS FULL OF CLOTHES. I WAS ABOUT TO grab my bike when I spotted a newspaper someone had dropped on the sidewalk.

"What's it say?" Jacob asked as I picked it up and flicked through it.

"Um," I said, "every single article's about rabbits. *How to pamper your rabbit. Five snacks that drive your rabbits wild. Seven reasons rabbits are the best friend you'll ever have...* and the paper's got a new name too."

"What?" Zach asked.

"It's now called The Extraordinary Celebration Times."

"Good morning!" a tall man in a fishing hat boomed as he

strode toward us. The people behind him stopped in their tracks and began to follow him. "Have you read the news?" the man asked, nodding to the paper. "Have you heard?"

The people parroted his words until their voices grew into a rising chorus. "Have you read the news? Have you heard?"

"Yeah, we know what's going on," Zach said. He was about to cycle off when the man blocked his path.

"Do you want to hear something even more amazing?" the man asked. He continued before Zach could answer. "The great... nay, the astonishing Jepa Cloak has thrown his tent open today. At dawn no less! And everyone's welcome, young and old alike! Step right up and prepare to be bedazzled." Tears welled up in the man's eyes and rolled down to the folds of his smile. "Bedazzled!"

"Bedazzled!" The group behind him murmured.

"Sure," Zach said, "we'll be there." And then, before the man could make a move, he cycled past him and jumped his bike off the curb and into the street.

I followed as the group's long shadows stretched out from behind me.

❧ 22 ❧

SPELLBOUND

"I'm ready," Emily called out from behind her door. We were waiting in the living room while she'd changed. Thankfully Violet wasn't home, which meant there were fewer people to see us in our ridiculous clothes.

Emily leaped out in a long blonde wig that almost reached her waist, and a pair of round purple sunglasses. She'd picked out a jet-black ski outfit even though it was July. I stared at her, trying to figure out what on earth she was thinking. *You're going to roast in that* was the only thing I could think to say, so I kept my mouth shut and didn't ask any questions. Maybe she thought it made her look like a ninja?

Jake and Zach had already changed into their disguises. So had I, and I wasn't exactly comfortable with my new look.

The blindingly white tennis shirt wasn't the worst part. Neither were the plaid shorts and sneakers. No, the worst thing about my disguise was the eye patch. Emily had plucked it from her prop box and handed it to me proudly but I was horrified. I tried to come up with excuses not to wear it but she'd insisted. Once it was in place she looked me up and down, "Nah, I can still kind of recognize you. I know..." She'd then rummaged through the box and produced a bright green contact lens. "Pop this over your good eye, then no one will suspect a thing," she chirped as I groaned and took the lens.

Zach had it the worst. He was decked out in a flat cap, wide red corduroy trousers and a black-and-white striped shirt. His fidgety fingers kept creeping up to the livid purple scar that Emily had painted down one side of his face with her *Movie Monster Magic* makeup kit. "I look like an angry farmer," he'd protested.

I'd thought Jacob had gotten off lightly when I saw Emily had handed him a nice looking suit, but when he tried it on it was clearly two sizes too large. All the other clothes she'd picked out were too tight, the suit was his only option, so he used the belt from his jeans to cinch the trousers up. Then, when he came out of the Zach's room and saw Emily tormenting us with the props from her prop box, he'd quickly rummaged around and found himself a nice wide-brimmed hat that hid most of his face.

He sat down smugly thinking he was safe, until Emily dropped a battered leather briefcase at his feet to round out his ensemble. He glanced down at it and sighed, seeming almost as uncomfortable with his new getup as I was with mine.

"You guys ready to do this?" Emily asked.

"Yep," Zach said, "I've never been readier."

I heard his nervousness and felt the same. All we had were these ridiculous disguises and the pendants Ophelia Draven had loaned us. Given what we were facing, it didn't seem like much.

"Then I guess we should go," Emily said and led us out of the house.

· · ·

Before we knew it we were stashing our bikes in the woods behind Jepa Cloak's tent. I could see the striped canvas through the branches, billowing in the breeze as the strings of lights surrounding it twinkled like a golden web.

A line of ten or so people stood outside the tent. They looked pretty normal as they waited there in the line, but not so much as they came out. A man emerged from the tent with a smile tugging his lips and his eyes staring ahead like he'd just seen something amazing. He walked with a spring in his step, as if he was half his age. "Yes!" he cried out, clenching his fists like his favorite team had just hit a home run. "Yes!" His voice echoed through the woods.

"Another one down." Zach gave the tent a worried glance. "So who's going first?"

"I will," Emily said. I could tell she was trying to be brave, but I heard her fear. I felt it too. It was like we were walking into a trap, like Jepa Cloak wanted us to come.

Emily had done well with the disguises, but then I suddenly started to worry that they made us stand out even more. But even if they did, it was too late to do anything about it now. The extraordinary celebration was hours away. Soon night would fall and the whole island would be under Jepa Cloak's control.

"Good luck, sis." Zach tugged his cap down, and adjusted Emily's wig for her.

She smiled and held her pendant up. "I'm not scared," she said, "I'll be back soon."

We waited in the trees as she strode out of the woods and got in line. No one noticed her, not even Cloak's weird followers as they stood outside the tent, guarding it like soldiers.

Finally it was Emily's turn to go inside. She cast a nervous glance back to where we waited and I crossed my fingers for her. And then she stepped through the tent's flap and vanished into darkness.

We waited in silence. Each of us watched the tent, wondering what was going on in there. The bad feeling I'd had for days grew even stronger.

Finally, Emily stumbled out and raced past the line of people, her head down. Once she was clear of the crowd, she hurried back into the trees.

"What did he look like?" Zach asked. "What did he say?"

Emily gazed at him. For a moment, it was like she was having trouble remembering who we were. "It's cloudy..."

"It's always cloudy, it's Whidbey Island!" Zach said, his voice taut and impatient.

"No, I mean in my mind," Emily said, "I can't... there was a man... I think. Everything was dark. As soon as I got inside the voice started. It wasn't as loud as before but it was there, right inside my head. I..." she dug into her pocket and pulled out her pendant. She gazed at it for a moment and nodded, like the memories were returning. "I had to take it off. It got too hot and there was... steam. As soon as I removed it the voice was even clearer in my mind, so I ran before he could work out who I was." She looked like she'd seen a ghost. "That's all I can remember. It was like a dream... or nightmare."

"Did you see him? Did you see Cloak?" Zach asked, "Was anyone else in there with him?"

"No. But the man inside the tent... he didn't seem real. And I don't think the voice was his either. It felt like it was coming from somewhere behind him. From the shadows."

"We need to get a better look," Zach said, "you go, Jacob." Then he glanced at me. "Or maybe you'd be better, Dylan."

"How about you go?" Jacob said to Zach.

"Stop arguing," Emily said.

She was right. She'd just gone in to see Cloak and she hadn't made a big deal about it. Before I could offer, Jacob nodded. "I'll do it." He straightened his tie, pulled his hat down, grabbed his briefcase and set off for the tent.

He looked unsteady when he returned, like someone trying to walk on an icy street. He set his briefcase on a log, flipped the catch open and stepped back as a cloud of steam billowed out. It was coming from the pendant inside.

"Wow!" Zach said, as he swiped his hand through the cloud.

"It didn't work for long." Jacob sounded distant, like Emily had, even though he hadn't been in there for half as long as she had. He adjusted his glasses and gave us a serious look. "That fortune teller's not a man."

"Is it a woman?" Zach asked.

"No," Jacob shook his head, "it's a machine, one that was made to look like a man. And yeah," he glanced at Emily, "the voice is definitely coming from the back of the tent. I think there's a hidden space back there. I tried to get a look but as soon as I got near it the pendant started smoking, big time. I had to stuff it into the briefcase and get out of there while I still could."

"Did anyone try and stop you from leaving?" I asked.

"Nope. But whoever was in the hidden room laughed and whispered, *You'll be back. When the extraordinary celebration begins.*"

"We need to find out who this Jepa Cloak is," Zach said. He glanced at me. "We have to see who's hiding in the secret room. Maybe..." his eyes gleamed, "maybe it's AI, you know, artificial intelligence. Maybe it's out of control. That could explain everything. Expect killer robots next...." he glanced at me all wide eyed, "You're the faster runner out of all of us, Dylan. Go take a look so we can settle this once and for all."

I almost told him *to go take a look,* but I knew he wouldn't. He'd stall, protest and call for a toss of the coin of doom, and our time was running out. I tucked the pendant inside my tennis shirt, took the eye patch from my pocket and slipped it back on. Great, I thought, now I only had one eye to see with. But the last thing I needed was for Cloak, Draven or any of their goons to spot me coming.

"Good luck," Emily said.

I nodded and hurried off before I could change my mind. I took a roundabout path through the trees so no one would see where the others were waiting, and stumbled out onto the track.

There were about fifteen people ahead of me and no one paid any attention when I got in the line. The guy ahead of the couple in front of me turned and asked if they'd ever seen Jepa Cloak before. They hadn't. "Oh," he said, his smile wide, "you're going to be spellbound! It's going to change your life!"

I glanced past him down the line where at least two other *random* people seemed to be doing the same thing. They had to be plants, stooges placed there to dampen any suspicion and convince people to go in and see their master. I hoped they'd overlooked me; the last thing I needed was any of them taking notice.

Thankfully no one approached or questioned me and I got closer and closer to the front of the line.

I watched as people strode into the tent and when they came out they all wore the same stupid grins. Some hollered, some jumped into the air and clenched their hands, but all of them walked away as if someone had just presented them with the secrets to the universe.

And then, just as it was my turn, the wind gusted down from the woods and shook the tent, making the entrance gape open like a dark mouth waiting to swallow me whole.

23

BEHIND THE CURTAIN

I jumped as a voice called out from the darkness that surrounded me.

"Are you ready?" It was a woman, hidden in the shadows. A spotlight flicked on and she stepped into its glow. She was tall and spindly. Her wide eyes blinked rapidly under her short fringe-like bangs as she gestured toward a narrow canvas corridor.

"I guess," I said, trying to make my voice lower, gruffer. "How much is it?" Suddenly I realized I didn't have a single dime on me.

She laughed. "Happiness doesn't cost a cent. The only thing we ask is that our patrons keep an open mind."

I bet you do, I thought. My fingers brushed the pendant. Would it work? According to Emily and Jacob it would, but not for long.

"What are you waiting for?" The woman smiled. "Your new life awaits. Go now. Listen and you'll hear the wisdom of the ages, spoken with truth and certainty by the great Jepa Cloak."

"Right," I said. The tunnel stretched into darkness, its

walls billowing softly. The only light I could make out was far ahead. It seemed to be coming from a flap-like door.

As I walked down the tunnel, I tried to figure out how long it would take to run back and get out, if I needed to.

"Go on!" the woman called from behind me. I'd almost forgotten she was there. My legs trembled as I fixed my gaze on the fluttering door and my heart thumped hard.

As I reached the last stretch, a light flashed above me, projecting glowing spirals on the tent walls and they spun around and around in circles.

"Welcome," a voice called from ahead. It was the same voice I'd heard before, the one that had wormed its way into my head, but now it seemed different. Like it hadn't quite worked out who I was yet. "Welcome to your new life." He sounded like one of the salespeople that hassled my parents every time we walked through the mall. Slick and as fake as a three-dollar bill.

My hand faltered as I reached out to pull the flap aside. I shook my head. Emily and Jacob had gone in and they'd come out alive. I could too. I had to. I was our last chance. There was no way Zach would ever make it this far, which meant it was up to me to find out where the voice was coming from and what it was.

Suddenly, as I pulled the curtain back, I felt warmth against my chest. It was coming from the pendant.

I peered into the opening. I couldn't make out how large the space was amid the darkness but it seemed hollow and vast, like a huge, empty cave.

In the middle of the shadowy murk, under the softly flickering yellow glow of a spotlight, sat a man at a polished wooden table. He wore red silken robes and his hands were curled tight around a glowing blue crystal ball. A turban towered over his tanned brow and his lips were set into a confident smile amid his sculpted black mustache and goatee. Glimmering beads hung from the pointed tips of the long dark beard, making his eerie face appear elongated.

"Welcome," he said. His voice was as soft as velvet and his huge brown eyes glimmered with pinpricks of light.

I tried to work out where his voice was coming from. It seemed to be somewhere behind him, just like Jacob had said, but I couldn't see past the spotlight.

"Please be seated." His head inclined mechanically to the chair in front of the table. As I sat down, the pendant grew even hotter. I reached up, running my finger along the chain until it found the position of the clasp. I wanted to know where it was, so I could take it off quickly if I needed to. "Let's begin," the man said. "Tell me, what is your name?"

"Andrew," I said, blurting out the first name that came to mind.

"Welcome, Andrew," the voice said. There was a pause. When he spoke again, it sounded like he was trying to disguise his irritation. "I sense a barrier, Andrew. Something blocking my insights and preventing me from connecting you with your most ideal and meaningful future. What is it?"

I gazed at the mechanical man as he twitched in his seat. Then his head inclined toward my chest as if he'd already knew the answer. Were there cameras or sensors in his eyes? I suddenly wished I'd hidden the pendant in my pocket. "I don't know," I said.

"Never mind," the voice continued, "together we will tear down these unseen barriers that are separating you from your destiny, Andrew. Now, tell me, what is your heart's desire?"

"I want to be rich," I said, blurting out the first thing I could think of.

"Oh I see riches ahead for you, Andrew. I see great, great things."

What is it you truly want? Who are you? Let me in, boy.

The voice slipped into my head. He sounded angry, and suddenly I realized he'd been whispering to me even while the mechanical man had been speaking. I grabbed the pendant. It was hot. Not unbearably, but it was getting there.

Take down your defenses. They're keeping you from true enlightenment. Let. Me. In!

I forced myself to stay focused. Everything he told me was lies. I was me, Dylan Wilde. I probably wasn't destined for greatness, not the kind people tended to imagine in daydreams but then again I might be. All I knew was that whatever I ended up achieving in my life, it wouldn't be down to Jepa Cloak. I scanned the gloom, trying to figure out where the voice was coming from.

Then I saw it; a tiny sliver of light in the darkness beyond the spotlight. That was where Jepa Cloak was hiding! Lurking in that crevice like a spider...

"The barrier between us is still present, Andrew." The mechanical hand rose up with a judder and pointed at my chest, right where the pendant was. "You must remove the charm if you wish to have your true potential revealed."

A dim silvery glow came from the hematite as it became as scorching as a sandy beach on a hot summer's day. I wanted to wrench it off, but it was the last defense I had, other than my own willpower. And it seemed like I had as little of that left as I had bravery.

But you *are* brave, I told myself. I could be, at least when it counted. Like now.

Why won't you listen to me? the voice cried out as it tried to sink right into my mind. *I've offered the carrot. Perhaps it's time for the stick... you're a weak, weak boy, Dylan. Yes, I see behind your disguise. I smell your fear and terror. The whole world frightens you, doesn't it? You pretend you're brave, but it's all for show, really you're as*

strong as a man of straw or jelly. Succumb, boy. Let me into your
thoughts. Now...

I felt my resistance crumbling away like a sand castle
engulfed by the tide. Any moment the voice would gain
control, and that would be the end of it. I'd be just like his
other followers; grinning, empty, lost. I had to expose Mr.
Cloak and fast.

"I am brave!" I said as I wrenched myself from the chair.
The mechanical man swiveled around as I ran past the desk.
He lunged at me but I leaped back and shot towards the
shadows where I'd seen the glimmer of light.

My hands trembled wildly and I winced as I tore back the
curtain.

❧ 24 ❧

UNMASKED

S tanding in a small tented room, surrounded by strange blinking machines, was a jackalope.

He was huge, far bigger than the one I'd seen in the woods. His eyes blazed bright, and his antlers were so long they vanished into the tent's shadowy peak. "No!" he cried. It was the same voice that had tried to get inside my mind. "No one must come back here!" He gave a slow, rasping growl.

The pendant burned and flashed with light. I tore it off and threw it at him as he thundered toward me, his massive feet thumping, his whiskers curled with fury.

"Carrot!" he shouted. "Carrot!"

For a moment I thought he wanted something to eat. Then I realized he was calling out for Ambrose Draven.

Something appeared in the darkness near his feet and as he shifted, I saw a tunnel stretching down into the earth. Then, in the glow of the string of gleaming lights that lined the chasm I saw Ambrose Draven racing up from the gloom.

I flew back through the tent. The mechanical fortune teller stuttered toward me. Behind, came a heavy thump of paws, and Ambrose Draven's furious cries.

Something swiped the air at my back. I turned to find myself staring into Jepa Cloak's blazing round eyes. I raced on, sprinting with everything I had, glad for all the times Jamie had tried to chase me down. If there was one thing I was good at, it was running.

"Boy!"

I stumbled through the tent flap into the long billowing corridor. The spirals of light flashed madly as they tried to hypnotize me.

Thump, thump, thump.

The ground shook as Jepa Cloak closed in on me. I could feel his breath on the back of my neck.

I had to make it to the doorway; I had to get out in the open. Then I'd be safe. He didn't want to be seen, he had to remain in the shadows. I fixed my panicked gaze on the fluttering canvas flap as the corridor seemed to grow to twice its length.

"Run!" I shouted to myself, like I needed telling.

Thump, thump, thump.

Suddenly, the scruff of my shirt was yanked back, pulling me with it. I reached up, shuddering as my flailing fingers brushed his furry paw. I pinched as hard as I could. With an angry growl he let go of the taut white cloth with a snap, propelling me forward.

I was almost at the end of the tunnel when the tall woman appeared. Her welcoming smile was gone and her face was filled with malice as she lunged for me. I feigned a left and dodged right.

Her hands almost got a hold of me but I slipped past and they closed on thin air.

Before I knew it, I was hurtling over the tangle of guide ropes and racing out from the darkness into the blinding light.

❧ 25 ❧

THE PLAN

My stomach lurched as I staggered out of the tent. The world spun and my feet tangled and tripped over themselves. I cried out as I slammed onto the trampled grassy ground.

The jackalope's eyes glimmered from the gloom of the tent, his pointed antlers jutted against the fabric wall, and for a moment I thought he was going to spring out and attack me. But then his gaze flitted from me to the waiting crowd and he pulled back and withdrew into the shadows.

Later, boy. His whisper hovered at the edge of my mind. *All I have to do is wait. Time is on my side.*

I scrambled to my feet. It looked like none of the people in the line had spotted Jepa Cloak. His followers, who were still pretending like they were there waiting to see Jepa too, seemed busy trying to distract the newbies. The others repositioned themselves, blocking the tent's entrance from view, no doubt in the hopes of keeping their dark secret hidden.

Then, three of Cloak's followers darted inside the marquee as if they'd been summoned.

I ran down the trail. I wanted to scream at the people who were waiting, I wanted to warn them. But it seemed the speakers outside the tent and the influence of the followers hidden amongst the crowd had already softened their minds. They were totally oblivious to the fact that I was there and no one even looked my way.

A cool breeze rattled the leaves as I raced into the cover of the trees, glancing back to make sure I wasn't being followed. I wasn't, not yet. As Cloak had said; time was on his side. He'd get me when it suited him.

"What happened?" Emily asked as I stumbled up to them. She looked worried, they all look worried. I told them everything.

"It's a jackalope!" I gasped. "A different one."

"Are you serious?"Jacob's eyes widened.

"Yeah," I said, "but this one's evil. The other one seemed to be good."

"Maybe that first jackalope was trying to warn you about this evil one," Zach said, "you said it spelled out danger in the dirt when you ran into it. Maybe-"

"Spelled? Hey!" Jacob shrieked, making me jump. A slow smile spread over his face. "Jepa Cloak! How could I have missed it?"

"Missed what?" Emily asked.

"Remember we all thought that was a really weird name... It's an anagram," Jacob said, "Jepa Cloak... *jackalope!*"

I spun the letters around in my mind. He was right.

"So that's why they've been renaming everything to rabbit related stuff," Jacob continued, "the streets in Langley, Ambrose Draven to Mr. Carrot... it all makes sense now."

"*Yeah, crazy* sense," Zach said.

"Sure," Jacob said, "crazy to us, but probably not to an unhinged jackalope."

"I didn't know they were mind readers," Zach said.

"Me neither," Jacob agreed, "but I'm no expert. I thought jackalopes were just a hoax until a couple of days ago."

"But what does it want?" Emily asked.

"Duh! To take over the island," Zach answered, "and Ambrose Draven is using his scientific know-how to help it."

"I figured that out already, thanks," Emily said, "I meant why here? Why Whidbey Island?"

"Who knows," Jacob said, "and it's not like we can ask him." He shook his head. "But now we know what it was that Ophelia Draven saw... and what tried to steal her mind. Her brother must have tried to introduce Cloak to her. That's why she's so paranoid."

"She's not paranoid if it actually happened," Emily said, "she was right."

"So how do we stop it?" I shivered as I gazed at the tent through the trees and saw the long line of people waiting expectantly for their moment with the robotic fortune teller. None the wiser to that creature lurking in the shadows...

"First we need to shut down the equipment that's broadcasting the signal, that's got to be how they're getting into everyone's minds so easily." Jacob turned to me. "We scouted out the clearing a bit more while you were inside the marquee. There's a small tent behind the main one. They must be storing something there, maybe the tech they're using to send the signal out to the speakers. Some of the papers you photographed in Draven's house looked like they were blueprints for some kind of amplifier but my guess is their signal only works on people who have been conned into hearing his message, otherwise we'd all be hearing it now."

"We need to shut it down," I said, "but how?"

"That's what Zach and I are about to try and figure out," Emily said. She didn't sound happy.

"We lost the flip of the coin of doom," Zach explained, his voice low. He kicked a stone, sending it thwacking into a tree trunk.

"We should all go together," I said, even though the last place I wanted to be was anywhere near that nightmarish tent.

"No," Jacob said, "you and me need to distract them so Zach and Em can get over there without being seen."

"Right." I didn't argue. Most of Jacob's ideas made total sense. He was one of the smartest kids I'd ever met, but I wasn't convinced that this was one of his better plans. It seemed like a bad idea. We needed to get help, maybe from someone off the island. This was too big a problem for us to face on our own.

"Are you with us?" Zach asked, as if reading my doubts.

"I don't know... maybe we should go back to the tree house and figure it out properly. You didn't see Cloak... he's terrifying!"

"There's no time for that," Jacob said, "the extraordinary celebration's hours away. Soon the whole island's going to be under Cloak's control."

I had more to say, but I held my tongue. The others seemed set on their plan, and what did I know, anyway?

But the bad feeling only got worse as Zach and Emily slipped off through the trees and Jacob hopped onto his bike. I watched as he pulled his hat off and tossed it over to where his briefcase lay on the ground. "Ready?" he asked.

I wasn't. It felt like everything was happening too fast. Like things were already out of control. But the plan was set. I pulled my eye patch off and chucked it down next to Jacob's stuff. "Sure."

We cycled through the woods and I followed close as Jacob zipped past the growing line outside the tent. "Go home!" he shouted to them.

"There's a monster in the tent!" I called as I cycled behind him. The crowd gave us lost, confused glances.

"Ignore them," said a woman as she sprung forward. She was one of Cloak's followers; I'd seen her guarding the tent earlier. "They're lying. The only monsters around here are these little brats. They're trying to steal your future from you, don't listen to them!"

I glanced away as Ambrose Draven emerged from the tent. He scowled as he lifted a huge sledge hammer up in his hand, then bounced the head of it on one of the massive tent spikes as he glared at me. Behind him, looming in the shadows was Jepa Cloak. He leaned down and whispered to Draven, and then they both vanished into the gloom.

Why?

Where were they going?

I turned to warn Jacob, but he was gone. I cast a panicked glance around for him and saw him racing away with two of Cloak's followers chasing after him.

As I turned back a giant, red-faced man stumbled toward me. "Come here, boy!" He growled like an angry bull as he charged at me. I planted my feet on the pedals and took off, glancing over as Draven and Jepa Cloak emerged from the rear of the tent and hurried off toward the trees.

Then, with a pang of icy terror, I knew exactly where they were going.

26

EVERYTHING YOU'VE EVER DREAMED OF

I cycled after Cloak and Draven, taking cover in the long looming shadow of the tent. The temperature dropped, and the color had faded from the grass, as if their towering, sinister big top was swallowing up everything around it.

"There," I said, gazing ahead.

Past the big marquee was a smaller tent set back toward the woods. It was tall but narrow and the top was shaped like a cone, as if it might be concealing a rocket ship that was waiting for its official unveiling.

Suddenly, the flap flew open and Jepa Cloak appeared. Emily and Zach walked behind him, dragging their feet like they were on their way to an execution. *Their* execution.

Behind them, Ambrose Draven followed, the big tent hammer cradled in the crook of his arm. My heart sank. I had to help them.

I glanced around for Jacob, but there was no sign of him. We'd been split up in the chaos.

Cloak stopped and held up a paw. The others halted behind him. He sniffed the air as I cycled toward them. A grin crossed

Cloak's face like a shadow, and his nose twitched. Then his eyes glowed and turned from brown to white.

He was using his powers.

"No!" I cried out as I felt his thoughts buzzing toward me like bees.

Come. Join your friends. Don't be afraid, boy. There's no fear underground, just warmth and happy darkness. Come to me; begin your new life with us.

I felt my head nodding in agreement. There was no point trying to fight him. He was going to take over the world no matter what I did. It was as certain as the sun rising, rainy wet weekends, and Jamie bullying me.

"Why fight?" I heard myself ask. It was as if the words were coming from someone else's mouth.

I fought to tear his thoughts from my mind.

"So be it." Cloak raised his other paw. For a moment I thought he was sending Draven after me, but instead Zach and Emily strode over. They didn't seem scared, not at all. Why?

"Hey, Dylan," Emily called.

"Are you okay?" I asked. Maybe Cloak hadn't gotten to them yet? Maybe he was letting them go?

"Don't be frightened." Zach smiled. "There's no reason to be, not anymore, Dylan. Everything's fine."

"It's so much better now," Emily said. "Come with us."

"Where?" I asked.

"Hey, Dylan," Emily said.

"Don't be frightened," Zach said.

My heart sank. They were on repeat. Cloak had gotten to them.

Zach inched toward me. I knew he going to try and grab me. "I'm sorry!" I called as I turned my bike in a tight half circle and raced off, leaving them behind.

The summer's warmth was gone. The day was cool and

dark. Ominous clouds gathered over the treetops as if they were preparing to smother us all.

I FELT TERRIBLE AS I CYCLED UP THE ROAD LEADING HOME. I'd left my friends behind. Who knew what Cloak might do to them now... I shuddered as I thought of the hammer cradled in Draven's arm.

Where had Jacob gone? I tried calling him but my phone was dead. I thought about calling him from the house but I didn't know his number by heart.

Wilson barked as I skidded to a stop and dropped my bike in the yard. I had to tell my parents everything. I had to stop them from going to the extraordinary celebration. They'd been weird last night and this morning too, but maybe there was still time to persuade them.

I needed allies. Badly.

"There he is!" Dad said as I hurried through the door. He grinned from where he sat on the sofa. Mom sat beside him, and Jamie perched on the edge of the armchair.

"Hi, buddy!" Jamie grinned too.

That was when I knew something was seriously wrong.

"You can't go to the celebration," I blurted, "you've got to stay away from Cloak. He's not who you think he is-"

"He was just here this afternoon," Mom said.

"Yes," Dad added, "and we're so glad he stopped by."

"Last night's consultation was amazing, but today we got an exclusive, private reading," Mom said. Her eyes gleamed but her gaze was empty and dull. "What a wonderful man!"

"But he's not a man," I said. "He's a jackalope. And a *con artist.*"

They gave no reaction, it was like they hadn't even heard me.

"We're going to be rich, Dylan." Dad's voice wobbled with excitement.

"Yep. We're going to need a much bigger house," Mom said.

"We're going to need more than one house," Jamie added.

I nodded dumbly. What else could I do? "That's great." I tried to sound excited.

"But before I forget," Mom said, "Mr. Cloak asked that you to go and see him, right away. He said it was urgent."

"Sure," I said. "Mr. Carrot already told me," I added, trying to see if they'd met Ambrose Draven too.

"Oh, isn't he wonderful!" Mom clapped her hands. "He came with Mr. Cloak. We're so lucky to have such sharp minds here on the island, what an amazing place it is!"

"Really," Jamie added and his smile was one of the strangest, sappiest things I'd ever seen. I realized if I got it on camera I could blackmail him into leaving me alone for the rest of my life, assuming we all lived through this. But unfortunately time was running out. "Yeah, they're great," I said, playing along, "I'm really looking forward to seeing them at the celebration."

"The *extraordinary* celebration," Dad added playfully.

"Yep," I nodded. I felt sick. I wanted to shake them, to scream the truth in their faces, but it was too late, they wouldn't want to hear it. They'd made up their minds. I forced myself to sound happy. "I'm going to take a shower and get ready."

"Good." Mom squeezed her hands and jittered like a kid waiting for their birthday presents. "I can't wait to hear what Jepa Cloak has to tell you, Dylan! I hope it's everything you've ever dreamed of."

"I'm sure it will be." And about as real as the money he promised you. I ruffled Wilson's ears as I headed for the stairs.

He seemed listless and down, like he knew something terrible was going to happen.

As soon as I got to my room, I fired up my laptop and plugged my phone in. I needed a number for the nearest police station that wasn't on the island. Everyone had seemed normal when we'd gone to the mainland, so there had to be someone there who could help. The only thing I needed to figure out was how to explain the situation without it sounding like some kind of crazy prank call. I watched the spinning wheel on my laptop and as soon as it finally booted, I opened a browser window.

"What the-"

A giant bright orange carrot framed against a deep blue background appeared on the screen. Then, two white eyes and a big sickle-shaped grin opened in its face. "Have I got news for you, Dylan!" the carrot said. I opened a fresh tab, and then another. The carrot appeared on each one. "Have I got news for you, Dylan!" they said, over and over.

I ran down the hall and grabbed the spare phone from Mom and Dad's room. I searched through the address book and tried calling my aunt and uncle. Their phone rung and rung, then someone picked up. "Hey!" I said. "It's Dylan. I really need-"

The sound of someone munching a carrot filled the headset. I ended the call and tried again. The same thing happened. I tried calling 911, but no matter what number I dialed, all I could hear was crunching carrots.

I threw the phone on the bed.

It was too late. Jepa Cloak had won. It was just me now, and maybe Jacob. If they hadn't gotten to him too.

27

NIGHTFALL

L aughter and voices drifted in from outside as I sat slumped on my bed. I had no idea what time it was, but the day was dimming and the heavy clouds made it darker still. I glanced out the window.

A group of neighbors were walking down the dirt track, carrying flaming torches. The firelight cast a red and orange glow on their faces. Then I saw the bunny ears fastened to their heads. They walked like zombies.

Someone laughed downstairs. It wasn't a normal laugh, and I didn't recognize it. My heart pounded as I slipped from my room and took a couple of steps down the staircase.

I glanced around the banister.

Wilson sat in the middle of the floor, growling, his ears high and alert. The living room was empty. There was no one there.

But someone had to be... I could feel it.

I almost jumped out of my skin as Dad sprung up from behind the sofa. He was hunched down, hopping like a rabbit, his nose twitching, his two front teeth bared.

The laughter came again, and then Mom appeared,

following him. She was crouched too with her hands held out as she hopped on her feet.

I snuck down the stairs as quietly as possible. Where was Jamie? I had to know...

He was sitting in the corner, his face glowing by the light of the television. A huge white spiral spun on the screen, and behind it I could see the same bright orange carrot that had appeared on my browser. Its eyes opened as I watched and a slow, nasty smile spread across its cartoon face.

I shivered as my phone rang upstairs in my room. I'd forgotten I'd left it charging... Mom and Dad glanced up the stairs. I pulled back, hoping they hadn't seen me as I slipped back to my room.

"Hello?" I answered the phone without checking who was calling.

"Dylan!" Emily said. She sounded excited.

"Are you okay?" I asked. Maybe they'd gotten away, maybe they'd somehow managed to get Cloak out of their minds...

"Hey, Dylan!" Zach's voice called out from the background.

"Where are you? Did you get away?" I asked.

"We're fine," Emily said, "we're just calling to see where you want to meet."

"Meet for what?" I asked, but a heavy sinking feeling passed through me as I realized what was coming next.

"The extraordinary celebration!" Emily said, chiding me like I should have known.

"It's starting in an hour," Zach added. "We'll meet you outside the fire station, alright?"

"Right." I ended the call. I phoned Jacob, but he didn't pick up. Everyone had turned. It was just me, and possibly Jacob left. The whole island, my family, and best friends were gone.

"I should join them," I said, my voice breaking. It would

be easy enough. All I had to do was go downstairs and attend the celebration with Mom and Dad. Maybe, if I handed myself in now, Cloak would let me join them without punishing me.

It was all he'd wanted; for everyone to be under his control. It felt like it was going to happen one way or another anyway, so why make it hard for myself? Everyone seemed a lot happier, that was for certain. Surely that wasn't a bad thing? And maybe Cloak hadn't been lying; maybe he could make us rich and important. Did I really want to throw that opportunity away? Did I really want to take this stand on my own?

"It's too late," I whispered. It had all happened so fast.

How could I go against someone as strong as Cloak? "I can't," I said as I caught sight of myself in the mirror. My face was pale, my eyes ringed with shadows from the last few sleepless nights. "What good have I done anyway?"

As I walked toward the door to join Mom and Dad, my gaze fell on the photograph hanging over my desk. Me, Mom, Dad, Jamie and Wilson. The picture was from two Christmas's ago. We looked happy. We'd been happy. Even Jamie had been half human for a few days.

They all looked so much happier now, but it wasn't real.

"He's lied to them," I said, "he just told them what they wanted to hear, but none of it's true."

I remembered a few days back when Mom had told me off for being too easily influenced. She'd said I needed to think for myself, and she'd been righter than she could have known. I couldn't abandon her and everyone else in the darkness with Jepa Cloak. We had to fight back. Me and Jacob. Or just me if it came to it.

But as I slipped quietly down the stairs, my resolve began to crack.

The living room was empty now. Even Jamie had gone, and the television was off.

Where were they? And how come-

Mom's head popped up over the sofa.

Then Dad, then Jamie.

They wrinkled their noses and bared their front teeth. Their shrill laugher was the most horrible sound I'd ever heard.

"Are we all ready for the extraordinary celebration?" they asked, their voices creepily in sync.

"Sure." I strode down the rest of the steps like it was no big deal. "I just have to run a quick errand first."

"Where are you going?" Mom asked.

"I... I have to get some fresh carrots to take with me; Mr. Cloak said he needs them right away." I continued across the living room carpet, leaving as much space between me and them as possible.

"Jepa Cloak spoke to you directly?" Dad sounded impressed.

"Yeah." I hated lying to them but there was no choice. "He said I need to hurry, so I'll see you there. Okay?"

They glanced at each other and twitched their noses.

"See you at the extraordinary celebration!" they cried, before vanishing back behind the sofa.

Wilson gave me a seriously concerned look as he cowered on his dog bed. I crouched down and scratched behind his ears until he seemed to relax.

"It's going to be okay," I whispered.

But as I headed out into the night, I wasn't sure if my words had been meant for Wilson or myself.

❧ 28 ❧

THE SINISTER PARADE

I flew down the trail as the treetops whipped by beneath the darkening sky. A weird blue light cast itself over the clouds. The world around me looked so unreal, almost like a starkly inked panel in a comic book. It was eerie. As if things weren't eerie enough already.

"Please be home," I gasped as I pedaled hard to get up the rise. I wasn't sure what I'd do if Jacob wasn't there. I didn't know, if push came to shove, that I could face Jepa Cloak on my own.

Suddenly, a line of rabbits bounded across the road. I slammed on my brakes. Where were they coming from? I watched as they flitted into the gloom and vanished from view.

Jacob's house was big, the only one in his whole neighborhood that was two stories high. It was tucked snuggly amongst a tidy yard halfway along a short road lined with neat little wooden houses. Thankfully, the lights were on and I could see his parents standing in their living room. I'd only met them once, along with his sister Gwendolyn, and I'd liked all three of them. They were really nice, easygoing and smart like Jacob.

Not every family gets stuck with a lemon like Jamie, I thought, watching them as they gazed out at the stars. It didn't seem like they'd seen me. Maybe, I thought, they hadn't been turned yet...

Then Gwendolyn's nose twitched, and her mother's did too. They started laughing as they gazed up at the sky. It sounded just like my parent's laughter from earlier. Totally insane.

I leaned my bike against the fence and ducked low as I snuck through the gate and followed the narrow path along the side of the house.

Jacob's bedroom was upstairs and his light glowed golden yellow in the strange inky blue twilight. I hoped he was up there and that they hadn't gotten to him yet. I called his phone, but he didn't pick up.

I thought about tossing a pebble at his window but I was worried it might break the glass. There was nothing else to do but climb. I reached into the heavy ivy running up the trellis on the back wall of his house and, with a few slips and curses, pulled myself up and peeked through his window.

Jacob was standing in the middle of his tidy, orderly room, staring at the monitor on his desk. His office chair was spinning just behind him and the screen was covered with cartoon carrots that looked like they were laughing at him.

Had they gotten to him too?

Suddenly he straightened his glasses, leaned down and hit the keys on his keyboard, closing the pop-ups one by one.

Surely he wouldn't do that if he'd already turned?

I pulled one hand free of the ivy, letting go just long enough to knock on his window.

Jacob jumped like a cat and spun around. He looked seriously relieved when he saw it was me and quickly opened the window.

"I just saw your mom and dad," I whispered as I climbed into his room.

He seemed terrified and his voice was raw and clogged with anger and sadness as he said, "They went to see Jepa before I got home. He's turned them."

"My parents too. And everyone else," I said, "I think it's just us now. We're the only ones whose minds are still free."

"Yep," Jacob agreed, "I was trying to search for help online, but our internet's down."

"Yeah, mine is too."

"I don't know what to do, Dylan." He shook his head.

That was bad. Usually he knew exactly what to do. I needed his help, needed him to start thinking. I knew where he was coming from but I also knew only too well that worrying would only make things worse. "I think we need to finish what Zach and Emily started," I said. "We have to break the signal Cloak's broadcasting from the tent."

"Sure. But we don't have any way of blocking it," Jacob said. "As soon as we get near the tent, he'll hypnotize us too, and then..." his words faded and his gaze fell on his bookshelf. A slow, half smile tugged his lips as he grabbed a pair of ear buds from his music player. "Maybe we can block his voice with these."

"Yeah! If we can't hear him..."

"He can't get into our heads. Have you got any with you?"

"Nope."

"Hold on, I'll see if I've got spares." He hunched over his computer, tapped some keys and brought up a spreadsheet on the screen. His eyes scanned the list then he leaped out of his chair.

"You keep spreadsheets of all your stuff?" I wasn't sure if I found that sad or impressive.

"Of course I do. I keep spreadsheets of everything!" Jacob

grinned as he pulled a large plastic box from under his bed and opened it carefully. A moment later he held up a pair of ear buds with a neatly coiled cord.

"Thanks." I said as I took them from him. "They look brand new."

"I think it'll work, as long as we remember to blast the music as soon as we hear his voice. We should probably be wearing helmets and shin pads too."

"Shin pads?"

"I read a couple of articles before our internet went down," Jacob said. "Legend has it that people used to wear metal stove pipes on their legs when they were hunting jackalopes, so they wouldn't get gored by their antlers. I don't have any stove pipe lying around but I figured shin pads and helmets would work. We can stop by the sporting goods store in town."

"But we don't have any money," I said, "Emily's got it."

"I don't think anyone's going to be there to take the money anyway. Everyone's hypnotized."

"Isn't that...stealing?" It didn't seem like a very Jacob-like thing to suggest.

"No, we're just going to borrow them. We'll pay for them as soon as we can, or maybe we can just take them back when we're done. I think it would be dumb to risk going without some protection at least. And if the stuff gets..." he gulped, "punctured or gouged... or if anyone gets mad about us taking them... then we'll apologize and figure something out."

"Yeah, I guess I was more worried about the sharpness of his mind than his antlers," I said.

"Well, hopefully we won't run into him at all. Maybe Cloak and his followers will be too busy with the celebration."

"Right." I forced a smile but I was terrified, and I could see Jacob was too. But I couldn't let it get to me. I had to believe we stood a chance of turning things around. Without that hope all we had was ear buds and shin pads.

JACOB'S PARENTS WERE STILL GAZING AT THE SKY AS WE snuck out. We walked our bikes until we were out of sight, then we took off down the hill, our wheels whirring as we sped into Langley.

Soon, people were everywhere, many clutching burning torches. The flames cast their faces red and orange, and with deep, spooky shadows.

It looked like there was a street fair going on, but then I spotted that the vendors only had one thing for sale: carrots. There was carrot bread and carrot soup, carrot salad, carrot burgers, carrot noodles, and huge wedges of carrot cake. Most of the crowd was wearing the bunny ears that Cloak's strange, grinning followers were handing out.

"Look!" Jacob whispered, as he nodded up the hill on the other side of town.

A silhouette of a giant rabbit appeared, like it was levitating down the street. Massive antlers crowned its head and its eyes glowed soft white in the dusk. It took a moment to realize it was made of paper mache and that it wasn't floating along; it was mounted on the back of a flatbed truck like a parade float.

"He's acclimatizing them, getting them used to the idea of jackalopes," Jacob said, "that way they won't be shocked when they actually see him."

I nodded dumbly. To my mind the whole scene was turning into something out of a horror movie.

"He might have one of those amplifiers hidden inside that float of his too," Jacob continued, "that's what I'd have done."

"Well, it's a good thing you're on our side." I said as I glanced over at him.

The crowd began humming that weird, toneless sound I'd heard before. They held their hands up and waved them slowly toward the giant rabbit. Some held flickering lighters in the air as they swayed, then a small man with a wild mop of curly black hair started dancing, his angular face cocked to one side.

A wave of light burst out from the float illuminating the jackalope, revealing the giant pink Easter egg cradled in its paws. It was a clock, ticking down to the extraordinary celebration. It was starting in less than half an hour.

Welcome! Are you ready to celebrate the beginning of your new lives? Cloak's voice slithered out coolly from inside the paper mache jackalope, just as Jacob had predicted.

We crammed our ear buds into our ears and I hit play on my phone. Heavy guitars and a tattoo of drums kicked in. I couldn't remember who the band was, but the pounding music helped me cycle faster as Jacob and I took off down an alley.

Unlike most nights, all the shops were open late and their windows were brightly lit. As we passed by I could see the staff inside. They stood as stiff and still as mannequins as they stared out toward the street. When we reached the sports store, the doors were wide open and a surly teenage assistant stared blankly as we entered.

Jacob pulled one of his ear buds out, listened carefully, and then nodded for me to do the same. "Either the signal isn't strong enough to reach the store, or Cloak's not broadcasting right now," he whispered, "come on."

I followed him down an aisle of fishing equipment. The store was small, so it didn't take long to find the hockey gear at the back.

Jacob glanced over his shoulder, and then pulled down a selection of shin pads. We tried them on and I found a pair that fitted pretty well. I strapped them on over my jeans and then we tried the helmets.

"Put your ear buds back in first," Jacob advised. I did as he said, and soon the world was muffled. I felt better, protected even.

"Well, we've got our armor. Now it's time to face the dragon," Jacob said, raising his voice.

"Can I help you?"

The assistant was halfway down the aisle behind us and it seemed like he'd woken up. "Can I help you?" he asked again in the exact same tone he'd used before.

"Jepa Cloak sent us here to prepare for the extraordinary celebration!" Jacob answered, half shouting.

"Can I help you?"

Jacob nodded for me to run. We split. He ran down one aisle, I ran down the next. I was almost at the end when the assistant appeared before me. "Can I help you?"

I threw myself to the floor, skidding on the slick shin pads as I shot below his legs. Before he could turn, I jumped up and raced to the door.

Jacob was already on his bike. He held mine out as I leaped on the saddle.

We took off, heading out of town as the giant rabbit floated down the road and the flaming torches grew bright beneath the darkening sky.

Night was coming fast.

❦ 29 ❦

GOING UNDERGROUND

O ur bike lamps cast dim yellow beams onto the road, highlighting swirling swarms of mosquitoes. As I slapped one from the back of my neck, my hand bumped the side of the hockey helmet and a muffled thump filled my ears.

Everything looked and felt so strange. It was like we were cycling through someone else's dream, or nightmare. Except it was real, and it was all happening too fast. I shivered as I glanced into the woods beside the road. They were dark and filled with heavy, shifting pools of night.

"This way!" Jacob called as he turned down the narrow trail leading to the marquee. Yellow lights flickered in the distance, and behind them, I could just about make out the tent, a pitch black mountain in the darkness.

Jacob held up a hand and pulled his brakes, sending up a cloud of dust. I skidded up beside him. He popped his helmet off and handed it to me as he yanked one of his ear buds out to listen. He gestured for me to do the same.

"Cloak's not broadcasting here," Jacob said, "he's probably

channeling everything through that giant jackalope float in Langley. For now at least."

I glanced ahead. "It doesn't look like anyone's here. I guess they're all in town for the celebration." I gazed at the tent, relieved that it was still and quiet. "So we just need to find the amplifier and shut it down?"

Jacob nodded. "That should do it. I hope. Come on." He clipped his helmet back on and we cycled down the trail. Jacob pointed to the woods, left the dirt track and cycled into the trees. I did the same, and as I glanced back to the tent I saw a few of Cloak's followers silhouetted in the darkness outside the marquee, gazing up into the sky.

Twigs and branches cracked and snapped below our wheels. The sounds they made seemed loud, even with the ear buds in but none of Cloak's followers seemed to notice.

We cycled past the main tent and headed toward the smaller one, ditching our bikes in the brush when we were close.

As I started toward the cone-shaped tent, my hands turned clammy. Everything was resting on us, the fate of all these people, and our friends and family. It was too much; I had to put those thoughts out of my mind.

Jacob lifted the tent flap, glanced inside and gestured for me to follow him. The space was cramped. Most of it was taken up by a tall silver pole that reached up into the air. At its base, a mass of thick heavy wires snaked down into the earth and to one side sat a wheeled console with a large monitor. On the screen were four towering poles just like the one next to us, and they were all connected to a large black rectangle at the center of the diagram. "What is it?"

"I think it's the network." Jacob tapped the screen. "These towers are connected to an amplifier. That's how they're sending out the signal. It looks like there's four of them.

There's one hidden inside the jackalope float, and then there's this one here." He patted the silver pole. "That means there has to be two more somewhere."

"How are we going to find them?" I asked. "They could be anywhere."

Jacob shook his head. "We don't need to find them all, we just need to find the source, the hub, and shut it down." He nodded to the black rectangle. His determined smile faded as he glanced down at the thick cables snaking into the ground. He looked ill.

"What's wrong?"

"You see those? All this equipment is hard wired." His finger trembled as he pointed. "So that means the hub's got to be down there."

"Where?"

"Underground," he said, his face shining in the flashing monitor's sickly blue light.

❧ 30 ❧

A MOST EERIE PLACE

"Can't we just cut the wires?" I asked as I shone the light from my phone across the tangled nest of cables. Each of them vanished down into a large brass tube that seemed to plunge to the very depths of the earth.

"No way." Jacob tapped his finger on one of the wires. "I don't want to risk getting electrocuted, do you?"

I shook my head, surprised at his snippiness. Then I remembered what Emily had said about his fear of confined spaces. "Are you okay?"

"Sure." He forced a smile. "Let's go take a look at that hidden room in the big tent. You said you saw a tunnel in there, right?"

I nodded as I considered what I was about to say. "Just tell me what I'll need to do, I can go down there on my own, you know. You don't have to go with me." I wasn't exactly thrilled with the idea. I didn't have claustrophobia or anything, but the thought of going inside that creepy old tunnel alone made me feel sick.

Jacob held the tent flap open for me. "No way, Dylan, we're in this together." He nodded. "Come on."

We walked slowly around the large marquee. The woods were so dark, they looked like a big billowing curtain of black and the Christmas lights twinkled and swayed around us like a web of fallen stars.

I forced myself to stand tall. I had to be brave. For Jacob, and for everyone else caught under Jepa Cloak's spell.

The tent opening was fastened. It seemed to take forever to open it as I fumbled with the ties while Jacob kept watch. Finally, we slipped inside.

I tried not to shiver as I faced the dark tunnel leading to the fortune teller's chamber. I thumbed the flashlight app on my phone but Jacob covered it with his hand. "No lights," he whispered, "we don't know who's in there."

"Right." My voice wobbled as I slipped the phone back into my pocket.

We were halfway down the tunnel when the flashing spirals lit up the tent walls, turning in tight shimmering blue white circles.

"Don't look at them," Jacob mouthed to me.

My sneakers and shin pads glowed whitish blue as I stared down at my feet. Slowly, we continued, and then Jacob stopped outside the main chamber. I glanced back down the murky canvas tunnel to see if anyone was following us, but the coast was clear.

"Ready?" Jacob whispered. The tent was so quiet I could hear him, even with the ear buds and hockey helmet on.

"Sure," I lied.

He pulled the flap open and we stepped inside. The spotlight in the center still cast sickly yellow light down over the mechanical man. His hands were clamped around his crystal ball and his eyes were pools of blackness as they gazed down, like they might be reading some cryptic fortune. We crossed the chamber, leaving as much space between him and us as possible.

We'd almost reached the hidden room when I heard the long drawn-out squeak behind us.

Dread tumbled like icy drops down my spine.

The fortune teller's face had turned our way and his black eyes were trained right on us.

"Come on!" Jacob said.

We scurried into the hidden room.

I gazed down at the tunnel plummeting into the depths of the earth. The string of lights lining its dirt walls flickered and a cold breeze welled up over us, bringing with it a heavy earthy smell.

"Ready?" Jacob asked.

"Nope."

"Good, me too." He smiled as he clapped a hand on my shoulder. "In we go then. We've got this, Dylan."

"Right." I said.

"Just be ready to blast your music if you have to," Jacob held up his phone, his thumb hovering over the play button on his music app.

I nodded as together, we descended. The dirt floor was hard and compacted under long trails of footprints. Most were from sneakers, some were from shoes. But there were huge paw prints too.

The dim lights flickered and cast long, eerie shadows along the walls and as we passed a bend the temperature dropped. Suddenly I could see my breath fogging up in the air. Jacob glanced at me and then back the way we'd came. His face was graver than I'd ever seen it. His lips moved, as if he was talking to himself, but then he fixed his glasses in place and strode on.

The descent grew steeper, and as I gazed ahead, I spotted a

deep dug out recess. Jacob held up a hand, and we crept toward it for a closer look.

I almost cried out.

Standing inside, in an odd sort of muddle, were twenty or more people. They lurked in the darkness, staring down at the ground like they were waiting orders.

It was one of the creepiest sights I'd ever seen.

Jacob tip-toed inside, keeping as much distance between himself and Jepa's followers as possible. Then he examined the walls and ceiling, and I realized he was searching for the wires we'd seen in the tent above. He shook his head and crept back toward me. He looked like he wanted to run. I knew how he felt.

The tunnel continued steeply down then branched off into two directions. Light filled one, the other was as black as night.

"Which way-" I stopped as Jacob held his hand up again.

Voices echoed up from a glowing fork of the tunnel and shadows roved along its wall as a group of people rounded the bend.

They were heading right for us.

❧ 31 ❧

THE MACHINE

J acob grabbed me by the sleeve and pulled me with him as he scuttled into the dark tunnel.

I couldn't see a thing. A horrible whistling screech echoed down the passage, like a wind was blowing from the very center of the earth.

We stood just inside the mouth of the black yawning cavern, turning our backs toward its blinding depths as we waited to see who'd emerge from the tunnel next to ours. I tried not to breathe, hoping they wouldn't notice us, hoping they wouldn't hear. Hoping over and over again that they'd simply pass us by.

The space at my back seemed to stretch out for miles, and I shuddered as images of grasping hands reaching out from the impenetrable darkness filled my mind.

Jacob froze as three figures shuffled by, heading along the tunnel leading to the tent. It took a moment to recognize them. Myron Draven, Cora and that meat head Eugene. They shuffled with slow, uncertain steps, and then Myron spoke. "The celebration is about to begin," he said. Eugene and Cora repeated his words in the same hushed, dull tone.

Then more followers emerged from the passage. Then more still. Soon there were at least fifty people walking up the tunnel toward the tent. Flaming torches flickered in their hands and their voices echoed as they said, "The celebration is about to begin."

Something skittered behind us. Was it coming our way? My skin crawled, and it took everything I had not to flee out into the passage.

Finally, the last of the shadows vanished. We hurried out from the gloom and stood under the lights. When I glanced back, I swore I saw glinting eyes, but they disappeared. "Which way now?" I asked.

Then, as I saw Jacob's face in the light, my spirits sank. He looked nauseous, withdrawn and he seemed to be mumbling to himself. He caught me watching and hurried on. "Come on," he said, his voice short again.

We passed a bend and stopped next to another dug-out burrow set back into the earth. I glanced inside, expecting to find more people lurking in there, but it was filled with big wooden crates packed with carrots. There were so many of them that the place smelled like one giant carrot.

I turned to speak to Jacob. He wasn't there. I scrambled along the tunnel and found him standing ahead, staring down toward where the tunnel dipped. He was gasping for breath and beads of sweat glimmered on his forehead.

"You need to get out of here, go back up," I said.

"I can't leave you here." His voice was hoarse and his fingers trembled as he wiped the sweat from his face.

"You can," I said. The thought of being alone in this dank, hideous place terrified me, but I couldn't stand seeing him like that. He looked like he was about to break. "Look, I can shut the machines down if you tell me how. I don't need you with me."

"Okay, find the power source. Then you can shut everything down. Hopefully that'll disrupt Cloak's messages and get everything back to normal. We need to buy ourselves more time, but-"

We froze as a voice muttered from the bend in the tunnel and a long shadow fell across the dirt floor. I recognized the mad wiry hair straight away. Ambrose Draven.

A moment later he appeared carrying a silver case. Unlike Myron and the others, he didn't seem to be hypnotized, which meant he'd spot us right away.

"Go, Jacob!" I shoved him back the way we'd came.

He stumbled then sank to his knees as he took a deep, unsteady breath. I could see he was struggling to decide what to do. I glanced back down the tunnel. Draven still hadn't seen us, but we had seconds at best until he did.

"Go back. Hide in the carrot room!" Jacob said.

"No, you've got to get out of here!" I whispered.

"I will. But you need to hide. Now!" Jacob pushed me back toward the doorway. I ducked inside and watched from behind a crate as he glanced up and down the tunnel. "Hey, Carrot!" he called.

"You!" I heard Draven growl. Then his shadow appeared on the wall and I could tell he was running.

"Good luck!" Jacob whispered as he raced off. A moment later Draven flashed by, his hair snapping around his head.

I waited for a second before sneaking out and peering around the doorway. Draven was running hard, and I caught a flashing glimpse of Jacob's shin pads and sneakers as he vanished up the tunnel's curve.

Draven was already slowing, which meant Jacob should make it out with no problem. I was happy until I realized that I was now completely on my own.

I thought about making a run for it too, of being back

under the stars in the fresh air and away from the endless shadows and the mossy scent of dirt.

"This is probably what it's like just before you get buried alive," I muttered as I looked at the walls around me. I shook my head, irritated by my runaway imagination. Now wasn't the time.

A voice echoed down from above. Draven? He sounded angrier than ever.

I hoped Jacob was safe. He'd come all the way down into the tunnel, despite his phobia. Somehow he'd contained his fears. I needed to do the same. I ran down the passage, my shin pads rubbing against my jeans, the helmet shifting on my head. Armor for facing the dragon, as Jacob had said. I had to remember that.

The tunnel leveled out then took a sharp bend. Murky shadows, cast by the dim lights, danced on the earthen walls.

I turned the corner and slowed before the large opening ahead. Lights flashed in the gloom beyond. It had to be where Draven was storing his devices...

The burrow they'd dug out for it seemed to be enormous, its ceiling so high it vanished into the shadows, its walls lost to the gloom surrounding it. The only light came from the metal racks loaded with flashing black boxes. Their long wires and thousands of flickering LEDs stretched back into cavern.

In the midst of it all was a huge square machine with four golden brass-like metal antennas stretching up into the darkness. There was a sudden low hiss and I jumped as crackles of pulsing bright purple light ran up the antennas and into the gloom above me.

Next to the machine was a control panel, dozens of monitors, and a massive metal arch, that looked like an airport security gate. The sight of it made my flesh creep. I didn't know why, but I just knew it was something terrible.

I glanced around. It seemed I was alone, but I couldn't see past the shadows gathering at the edges of the machinery.

Anyone could be lurking there...

"No." I couldn't let fear stop me, I had to focus.

I watched the monitors as their screens flashed with scrolling lines of green code. I had to shut them down. I glanced around; searching for the power supply, but the wires and cables from the machines vanished into the shadows. As I gazed into them, it felt like someone was standing in the darkness, watching me. "You've got this," I whispered to myself as I took a hesitant step forward.

And then someone grabbed my shoulders, freezing me in place.

32

LOST RABBITS

My heart felt like it was in my throat as I spun around. It was Zach, right behind me, his hand clenching my shoulder. Then, Emily appeared from the murk.

"We told him you'd come," Zach said.

"Let go," I said, "I need to turn the-"

"No." Emily shook her head. "You need to stop, Dylan."

"She's right," Zach said, "stop sneaking around in the shadows. Stop fighting him!"

"Let him show you the path," Emily said, "your new life's going to be amazing!"

"Everything's going to be amazing!" Zach added as his fingers dug into my bones.

I was about to shake him off and run from the chamber but then I stopped cold.

Cloak's followers blocked the entrance. It felt like their eyes were burning into me as one by one they grinned. Then they parted as a dark shadow fell across the tunnel behind them. It was tall and broad with a giant rabbit's head and black snaking antlers that seemed to stretch out for me.

"You should listen to your friends," Jepa Cloak said, as he walked past his crowd of followers and stood before me. He pulled a pocket watch out from under his fur. "Oh dear! I shall be late!" His laugh was like a boom of thunder. "But I'm mistaken. You're the one who's going to be late, Dylan Wylde. Late for this world!"

"Let me go!" I wrenched myself away from Zach.

Jepa Cloak's nose twitched and his eyes widened like dark pools that were going to swallow me up. "Why are you being so difficult?" he asked "why won't you give in to your destiny? Look how happy my followers are. Don't you want to be happy too, Dylan?"

"They're not happy," I said. "They just think they are. You've lied to them, fooled them. You've fooled everyone!"

"Maybe." Cloak folded his great furry paws over his chest. "But one can only fool those who wish to be fooled. And who's more content right now, you or them?"

Let me in. His voice appeared at the edge of my mind.

I reached for the pendant but realized it wasn't there. I didn't have it. I didn't have anything.

Obey. It's the only way.

I shook my head. "No!"

"Perhaps," Cloak said slowly, "you'd be happier joining the other lost little rabbits."

"Lost rabbits," Zach and Emily said. Then the rest of the crowd repeated it. They sounded terrified as they huddled together.

"That's the fate of those who refuse my call," Cloak said. "Do you want to know what happens to the lost rabbits, Dylan?"

"Nope." I forced down the scream building in my throat.

"Let me show you." Cloak turned to his followers and gestured for a hunched old man with silvery-white hair to come forward. His movements were slow and timid. "Out of everyone here you've done the least for the cause, Max," Cloak said. "If I remember right, you managed to add a paltry seventeen followers to my colony. That's the lowest recruitment score in the burrow. And you know what happens to losers; they become lost rabbits. Hop through the gate, Max. Don't tarry!" Cloak bounded over to the bank of monitors and thumped his paw down upon a big round red button.

I flinched as the silver gateway gave a metallic clang and pulsed with crackles of blue and gold bolts of electricity. Power surged around the arch, building and building in volume as the monitors and tiny lights dimmed, winked and flickered in the cavernous room. Were all those recent power outages down to this horrible machine?

"I told you not to lollygag." Cloak bore down on Max. The old man nodded and clasped his hands together as he stepped toward the arch and with a sharp shove of Cloak's great furry paw Max stumbled in.

Suddenly, there was a flash of lime-green light and clouds of smoke belched from the vents on the sides of the arch. I thought I heard a gasp and then a screech, but it might have been the machinery.

When the smoke thinned, Max was gone and in his place was a tiny, frail white rabbit.

"Shoo now, Max!" Cloak growled as the little white fuzzball scurried through the leggy maze of followers and fled along the tunnel. Cloak turned back to me. "So what's it to be, Dylan? A new gilded life in the burrow, or would you prefer to take your chances as a lost rabbit, hunted and alone in the dark?"

I couldn't hold his stare. As I looked away, I noticed the others watching. They were hanging on to Cloak's every word.

He was proving his strength to them by exposing my weakness.

He seemed to read my thoughts as he nodded to the shadows, and a moment later my parents and Jamie stepped into the light. Then, someone else moved up alongside them. It was Jacob. He adjusted his glasses over his dull eyes. "Let him into your life," he said, "it makes perfect sense."

My mom cocked her head, like she was listening intently to something I couldn't hear. "You'll be so much happier, Dylan."

Dad's eyes glistened as he said, "Don't become a lost rabbit."

Then, Jamie smiled at me like we were old friends and not sworn enemies. "I'm sorry I was so mean to you, bro. I never realized how amazing you are."

I shook my head. The Jamie I knew would never say that. Cloak was speaking through them. He was using their mouths to speak his lies.

Let me in! Cloak screamed. I slipped my hand into my pocket, ready to hit play on my music app.

Cloak's eyes glowed white, and then everyone else's did too. It was a spooky, horrible scene.

Maybe I should give in... it would be so much easier... I didn't want to be alone. I didn't want to become a lost rabbit. I shivered as I thought of all the rabbits wandering through town. There were so many... who would ever notice me, who would even remember me?

Let me in now!

I glanced at Mom, Dad, Jamie, Jacob, Zach and Emily.

They looked so happy. But it was a lie. He'd snuck into their minds when they weren't paying attention. They weren't really living their own lives or thinking their own thoughts, it was all lies. None of it was real.

"No." I turned on Cloak. Let him do his worst, I thought, I

wasn't giving in. If I stood up to him, then maybe everyone else would start to see the truth and do the same thing.

"Obey!" a voice growled. Ambrose Draven stumbled through the doorway, his tent hammer cradled in his arms.

I staggered back as he lurched toward me, his eyes furious, his hammer raised to squash me.

"No!" Jepa Cloak said, looking around quickly as his followers watched us.

Draven paused.

"Bring the boy to me. Unscathed."

"But..." Draven shrugged, "he's defying you."

"We do not harm," Cloak said, "we educate. Bring him here!"

"Come to me," Draven said, pointing at the floor before him. "Now. Stop challenging the master's wishes," he screamed, his voice echoing in the chamber.

"He might be your master, but he's not mine," I said.

This seemed to make Draven madder than ever. He growled like a grizzly bear and stumbled at me, his hands reaching out.

I ducked and shoved him away. He sprawled back and his arms flailed as he shouted and stumbled into the crackling arch. There was a thunderous boom and a bitter green cloud of smoke. As it wafted away an angry-looking little mustard-colored rabbit rose up on its hind legs.

"How dare you!" Jepa Cloak growled.

Then he strode at me, his teeth bared with murderous rage.

✿ 33 ✿

WHISPERS

The crowd from the tunnel swarmed me. I staggered back as they reached out to pat my shoulders and whisper, "Obey!" It was like they were trying to spare me from Cloak's fury.

He leaned in and his long ears trembled as a slow, sly smile passed across his tiny mouth. "Why are you wearing those ridiculous shin pads?" he asked, his voice shifting from anger to mockery.

I shrugged.

"Were you afraid I'd gore you with my antlers like the legendary jackalopes of old?" Cloak laughed. "I've no need to resort to violence, Dylan. I'm not here to wound, I only wish to heal." He turned to his followers. "Isn't that so?"

"It is so," they echoed back.

He waved his paw toward them, and gave a fake, sentimental smile.

I knew what he was doing; he was pointing out how many more of them there were compared to me. How I was all on my own. How it was me, alone, against everyone else.

That's right, he whispered at the edge of my mind, *you're all alone. But there's still time to change your foolish decision, my boy. Let me in. Give up now and be free. You won't worry anymore; you won't need to think about a single thing. Join my colony and everything will be taken care of for you.*

I almost agreed as I gazed at the crowd's expectant, watchful faces. I didn't want to lose my family and friends. I didn't want to be separated from the people I loved.

But then, as I glanced at Mom, I remembered what she'd said that day when Jamie had tricked me into trespassing into Mr. Flittermouse's garden. About how I let others influence me. She'd been right, and this was no different...

"Do it, Dylan," Jacob said as I met his gaze. "Obey."

"Why'd you give in, Jacob? Tell me." I asked.

His brow furrowed, like he was trying to remember something from years back. "I... I was frightened. It felt like the earth was closing in on me, like I was being buried alive. Mr. Cloak took the fear away."

"And showed us our true potential," Zach added. "People will take us seriously now."

"Join us." Emily smiled. "Everything you've ever worried about goes away."

"No, it doesn't, it's all lies." I muttered. Then I was suddenly aware of Jepa Cloak studying me. Why hadn't he mounted his attack while I was distracted? Why hadn't he thrown me into the machine and turned me into a lost rabbit? Why was he hiding in tents and murky burrows?

Just give up, boy. All is lost for you now. You're stuck in the maze of your doubts, but I'll guide you to the exit. All you need to do is take down those silly defenses and help me to help you.

"Why are you whispering?" I asked, raising my voice. "Why don't you just say what you've got to say? Why don't you speak out loud? Are you afraid they might hear how desperate you are?"

Stop it.

Either his voice had grown quieter, or my anger had dampened it. And it might have been my imagination, but suddenly he seemed a little smaller. "You're like Billy Russey."

"Who?" Cloak demanded.

"My friend back in fourth grade. Or so I thought. He told me I was so smart and funny. Then, once we started hanging out he tried to get me to steal the teacher's purse for him. When I refused, he turned on me. He told the other kids lies about me to make me look bad. So I stopped talking to him, and he couldn't handle it."

I took a deep breath as I remembered what Billy had done afterwards. "He was so desperate for me to be his friend that he begged me. But I ignored him and that really upset him. A few days later he had a meltdown in front of the whole class. He started crying and then he admitted he'd made up the stories about me. He tried so hard to convince me he was my friend but he was a sneaky, insecure, bullying liar, just like you are."

Cloak's antlers glowed in the machine's purple light as he lifted his head high. His eyes shone, and the crowd stepped nervously away. "How. Dare. You!"

"Can't you see?" I turned to my parents. "He's not helping anyone. He's using you. Everything he's promised is a lie."

"How dare you!" Cloak thundered again and his eyes shone pure white.

He was about to lose his temper, just like Billy had. I'd gotten into his head instead of him getting into mine.

Could I do it again?

Could I get into Jepa Cloak's head? Did it work both ways?

Let me in!

🎐 34 🎐

BOOM!

Cloak's voice whined like an angry mosquito right at the edge of my mind. I hit play on my music app. Heavy guitars and snare drums kicked in as I watched Cloak shouting and gesturing in fury.

I was terrified, even though I knew what he was; a control freak having a tantrum. I forced myself to laugh and his eyes flashed a violent shade of red. Finally, people were starting to see his real face. Then, before he could recover his composure, I turned the music off. "Why are you doing this?" I asked quickly as I tried to catch him off guard.

"Because I can!" He screamed.

A shocked sigh passed through the crowd.

"But why?" I pressed.

"Because," his voice trembled, "because I hate you!"

Another sigh filled the room and this time a flicker of doubt passed over the people's faces. Jepa Cloak's face twisted with even deeper anger, and as our eyes met they were almost level. It hadn't been my imagination before, he *was* getting smaller.

"What have I ever done to you?" I asked.

"You... you people! You think you're so special. Think you have the right to run everything. But why? Why can't a jackalope run things? Tell me that?"

"I don't know. Maybe a jackalope should run things. But not you, not after what you've done. How about that other jackalope I met..."

"Hidey?" He growled.

"I don't know his-"

"*Her* name. Her. My love."

"When I saw Hidey she was running away," I said. Cloak was still unhinged, and his anger seemed to be making the spell he'd cast over his followers wear off. Just a little. "She couldn't speak. Was that down to you?"

Cloak nodded.

"Why?"

"Because she had nothing constructive to say."

"Did she agree with all this?" I asked, waving a hand at the surrounding equipment. It seemed I'd found his weak spot.

"No. And she nagged me to halt my plans. She was content to live under human rule, I was not."

"So you want to be king of the world?" I asked. "And no one can ever disagree with you?"

"Indeed."

"Well, you might get there, but you'll be all on your own. You'll have no one real to talk to. There'll just be a bunch of people around who will go along with whatever you say."

"Perfect!"

"Really?" I asked. "It might seem that way, but I couldn't think of anything more boring. You'll be alone. A lost rabbit just like the others."

"I'm not a rabbit!" he thundered.

"Okay, a lost jackalope."

His nose twitched and his eyes faded from white to brown. "Don't try to play games with me, boy."

"I'm not. I'm just giving you the last honest opinion you'll ever hear. After I'm gone, there won't be anyone left to tell you the things you don't want to hear."

"So?"

"So do you want to be alone?"

Cloak opened his mouth to say something, then closed it. He shook his head.

Another sigh ran through the crowd. It seemed like they were finally seeing Cloak for what he was, and the more he got angry, the clearer it became that his grasp on them was slipping.

"Do you have any idea how much work its taken to make this happen?" Cloak demanded. He gestured to the machines. "Do you know how hard its been, and how much of my powers its taken to win over so many people?"

"So what," I said, "it was a bad idea. You know it was. And it won't bring Hidey back either."

"It's too late," Cloak said.

"No it's not. Not yet."

His eyes flashed again and he lurched at me. His antler struck my helmet with a clunk and I fell to the ground.

"Let me in!" Cloak roared.

I stood and dusted my hands off. "No."

He looked like he wanted to tear me to shreds but then a stupid, sappy grin passed over his lips. "I've underestimated you, Dylan. You're easily the smartest boy I've ever met. And now I come to think of it, you'd make an ideal assistant. I could make you my vice admiral, perhaps."

"But I'm not that smart," I said. "And I'm not that dumb either. I'm just me."

His eyes flashed red and his antlers quivered as he bared his teeth. He'd lost and we both knew it.

Then, as he stared down at me, his gaze began to soften and his shoulders slumped. He shrunk down further and further, until his antlers were level with my knees. "All I wanted..." he swallowed and shrugged as he looked up at me. "All I wanted was a good life. That's all."

"And you can still have that," I said, "but you'll have to give up the idea of taking over the whole planet."

"Where will I live?" he demanded. "There's people everywhere I go. We jackalopes are not compatible, that's why I tried to make your kind compatible with us."

I thought for a moment. "What about the mountains? They're just over the water and there's probably not many people living up there. Mount Baker's not far. It looks pretty cold, but you have all that fur to keep you warm."

He gestured to his machines. "But look what I had Mr. Carrot... I mean Ambrose Draven build!"

"Like I said, it was a terrible idea. I've had plenty of them myself. Sometimes you just have to cut your losses and change course."

Cloak remained silent for a moment. "I wonder... I wonder if Hidey will come with me?" He nodded slowly. "I should never have silenced her." He glanced around, his eyes almost dreamy. "You know, I was really looking forward to world domination."

"I might have too, I suppose. But after a while I'd want everyone back to how they're supposed to be. Even Jamie."

"Very well." Cloak gave a heavy sigh. He wandered over to the control panel, leaped up on the side and began typing as the equipment crackled and hissed.

Cloak gazed at his followers, raised his paw and brought it down fast. "You're free," he said, his voice tired and forlorn.

He turned back to me. "It might take a few hours for them to be like their old selves again, but none of them will remember any of it." He watched as the crowd began to shuffle away like sleep walkers.

"That's probably a good thing," I said, "but you'll still need to take all of this down too." I gestured to his machines.

"That's doable. I have dynamite!" he said and his eyes glinted happily. "I can make it all go boom!"

"Yeah, as long as the place is empty first." I glanced at the flickering silver arch. "What about all the lost rabbits?"

"If I called them back, I suppose I could reverse the transformation." He sounded dejected as he sighed. It seemed he really had enjoyed being evil. Then, Jepa Cloak stuck two claws in his mouth and whistled. Within moments the place echoed with a loud, thunderous din.

"What's that?" I asked nervously.

"The lost rabbits," Cloak said.

We both looked around as the walls shook. It sounded like the whole burrow might collapse as the drumming grew louder and louder. Hundreds of shadows appeared on the floor of the tunnel.

Soon a tide of rabbits washed down the passage and hopped into the chamber. They surrounded Jepa Cloak in a wide furry circle, their beady eyes glinting, their noses twitching. He fired up the transformation machine and ushered them through its gate one by one.

Crackles and booms rang out, and soon the place filled with billowing white smoke.

The first to emerge was Ambrose Draven. He looked confused as he swept a hand through his mad hair. And then, as our eyes met, he hurried off up the tunnel. I had no idea how much of this was down to him, and how much was Cloak's masterplan, but it wasn't as if I could stop him, not then at least.

One by one the rabbits vanished and more people appeared, including Ophelia Draven who gave me a bewildered glance. Then I saw the old lady we'd been asked to look for on the beach. She gazed around the room and her son and daughter appeared from the crowd. All three looked baffled as they followed Cloak's pointing paw and quietly left the tunnel.

Soon the hoard of rabbits dwindled and the people left the chamber in droves. Once the last rabbit had transformed and most of the belching smoke had wafted away, a long shadow fell across the tunnel floor. I recognized Hidey as she hopped into the chamber.

"Hidey!" Jepa cried.

She glared down at him and raised a paw to her mouth.

"Right, right!" Jepa said. He muttered something I couldn't hear, and then Hidey opened her mouth and took a deep breath. Slowly, she began to shrink until they were both the same size.

A heavy silence fell over the chamber, and then she spoke. "You took my voice," she said. She sounded furious.

"I'm sorry." Cloak hung his head once more. "Really I am."

"Yes, you are," Hidey replied.

"Can you ever forgive me?" Cloak asked.

"We'll see." She turned to me. "Thank you."

"That's okay," I said.

"So we're free to go?" Cloak asked.

"Meet me on the beach in Langley at dawn. Just down the slope. Before anyone else is around," I said. "I need to discuss what happened with my friends in The Society of the Owl and Wolf, and see what they want to do next."

I turned and led the last of Cloak's followers out of the tunnels, including Emily, Zach, Jacob and my parents. For a moment I considered leaving Jamie there but I tapped his shoulder and he followed dumbly behind me.

As we emerged below the starry skies, I realized no one would remember anything that had happened. Not if I didn't tell them. I was tempted to keep it to myself. I didn't need to brag; I knew what I'd done.

I'd saved the world. Well, Weirdbey Island anyway.

TOP OF THE MOUNTAIN

We found Jacob's parents and his sister outside looking for him by the big tent. He strode over to them like nothing had happened. It didn't seem like anyone really knew what was going on or what had taken place. It was the same with Zach and Emily's parents and Violet, who wandered absently by the trail.

Once everyone had found each other, I followed Mom, Dad and Jamie to where they'd parked the car. It seemed Cloak had drawn the whole town to his burrow with his promise of the extraordinary celebration, and the meadow was jam packed with cars waiting to leave. It took ages to get home and crawl into bed.

MY ALARM WOKE ME EARLY THE NEXT MORNING. THE SKY was soft pink and gold in the light of the rising sun as I cycled to Zach and Emily's house.

I tapped on their bedroom windows until they finally got up. Zach looked outraged at first. But then he grew more and more excited as I told him we needed to get over to the beach quick, that something had happened and we needed to figure out what to do next. That The Society of the Owl and the Wolf needed to act. He hounded Emily, hurrying her along and we cycled by Jacob's place and got him too.

Then, we sat in the park while I told them everything that had happened. Soon, the tale jogged their memories as we discussed the whole chain of strange events.

"Where's Cloak now?" Zach demanded.

"He's supposed to meet us at the beach this morning," I said.

"And Ambrose Draven?" Emily asked.

"He escaped," I said. "I couldn't stop him on my own. Besides, I don't know how much of it was his idea and how much was Cloak's mind control. We'll ask Cloak when we see him."

"Draven will keep either way," Zach said.

Jacob nodded. He was quiet. Maybe it was too early for him, or perhaps that time spent in the confines of the tunnels was still gnawing away at him. I placed my hand on his shoulder and he smiled. "Thanks, Dylan."

We cycled together down the slope and shot across the sand, our wheels whirring, the early morning breeze sending our hair flying.

Jepa Cloak and Hidey stood on the beach. They watched in silence as we skidded in wide arcs and left our bikes resting on the sand. They'd both shrunk even more since I'd last seen them and now they were little bigger than garden rabbits. I wondered how much Cloak's magic had been responsible for their growth before, and how much of it was Ambrose Draven's meddling. They seemed uneasy, like they were waiting to see what we were going to say.

"Hi," I said, nodding to them.

"Good morning," Cloak said as he looked up at us one by one. "So have you decided what's to become of me?"

I glanced at the others and waited for them to speak.

"Where will you go?" Zach asked, "*if* we don't place you under arrest." He said it like he already had a rabbit prison picked out for Jepa Cloak.

Cloak pointed across the water, toward Mount Baker. "To the top of the mountain, if you let us."

"Uh, I think I'd prefer a home below the snow line," Hidey added pointedly and gave a slight shiver.

"Well," Emily said, "I don't expect the rest of the town will remember anything, apart from us. And the memory only came back to us because Dylan explained what happened."

Cloak nodded solemnly.

"How much of it was down to Ambrose Draven?" I asked.

"Plenty," said Hidey with a scowl.

"He certainly had a hand in it," Cloak said, "but ultimately I influenced him, just as I influenced everyone else. So... have you decided how I'm to be punished?"

"Well, we don't have any ways of holding you. And you pretty much set everything right. So we should probably let you go," Zach said, but he narrowed his eyes and I could tell he was giving things close consideration. "Although we could put you to work. Perhaps we could start a gardening business; those antlers could rake up a serious amount of leaves. Or, maybe we could hook you up to a treadmill and generator. You could probably power the whole island with those feet, and you did steal a lot of energy in your bid for world domination."

I wasn't sure if he was joking. Then Jacob met Cloak's dark, piercing eyes. "Do you swear to never use your powers on anyone again?" he asked.

"I do." Cloak held his head down. "I'm truly sorry."

"I believe you." Jacob said. Then he turned to the rest of us. "What do you think?"

"It's up to you," Emily said.

"No, it's up to us," Jacob replied. "We're the Society of the Owl and the Wolf now. All of us."

"I say let them go," Zach said, "even though we're losing out on some serious bucks. Imagine how much-"

"No get rich schemes, Zachary," Emily said. "That's not what this is about."

Jacob nodded and I agreed. Finally, Zach relented. "Fine."

"Thank you." Hidey said.

Jepa Cloak reached up and shook our hands in his paws. "I shall bid you adieu. So long," he said as they turned and began to scamper across the sand. Then, he looked back one final time, and his words whispered at the edge of my mind. *Thank you, Dylan,* he raised a paw, *you're stronger than you know. Remember that in times of trouble.* I nodded as I watched them bound away until they became tiny, distant dots.

WE SPENT MOST OF THE DAY IN THE TOWER OF ETERNAL Secrets picking over everything that had happened while Zach took plenty of notes. Once everything was properly recorded, we cycled to Mr. Ovalhide's house and turned in our first report as members of the Society of the Owl and the Wolf. Both Montgomery and his wife praised our success, while sneezing enough to start a small avalanche.

Then we passed the rest of the afternoon in the park, flopped out on the lawn watching people walking by. No one paid us any attention. It seemed none of them remembered a single thing.

Soon Zach started pushing for us to decide what to

investigate next but everyone, asides from him, thought it was probably a good idea to take a break.

LATER, AS I CYCLED HOME, A PAIR OF CHESTNUT-BROWN rabbits bolted across the road. They narrowed their eyes as I stopped, and gazed intently at me. But as I tiptoed towards them they shot off into the meadow.

I was about to pick my bike up when I heard a rustling in the long swaying grass. And then, as I looked again, I saw hundreds of beady eyes glinting back at me.

THE END

A PREVIEW OF BOOK THREE OF WEIRDBEY ISLAND - THE ISLAND SCAREGROUNDS

THE ISLAND SCAREGROUNDS

Chapter One

I ran hard. My chest grew tight and my arms and legs felt like they were full of lead.

It was right behind me.

I couldn't bring myself to look back. I didn't want to see it, I couldn't! But I heard it all the same.

Woosh!

I tried not to picture it, but it sprang into my mind like a jack-in-the-box. That long black cloak, the bone-white face, the ragged hood, the crooked silver scythe reflecting the red setting sun as if coated in blood. It was the Grim Reaper...

The woods and bushes seemed to grow denser as I ran. I'd been looking for an escape but it was almost like the surrounding trees were deliberately slowing me down so it could get me.

Whirrrr

I slowed, desperate to catch a breath, and gazed back.

It was floating above me, ten feet in the air, gazing down,

its eyes as red as the sunset. The ragged black cloak obscuring its bony body riffled in the breeze. *"Boyyyyyyyy!"* it hissed.

I plunged through the heavy brush, screaming as brambles snared my jeans and sleeves.

The whir of the Grim Reaper bellowed from somewhere to my right. It must have lost me for the time being.

I hunkered down behind a tree and my fingers sank into the spongy moss as I tried to catch my breath.

What was going on? Was death itself stalking me? Did things like that happen on a Tuesday afternoon in August? I guessed it happened all year round, but nothing made sense. I was sure it involved Jamie and Marshall, although I had no idea how. Maybe they'd found some dusty old grimoire that had helped them raise the Ghoul. It was unlikely, sure, but anything was possible since we'd moved to Weirdbey Island.

They'd been lurking on the road near our driveway when I was coming home from Jacob's. I'd been expecting them to say something mean or stupid, but before I reached them the Reaper had swept down from the sky, its shriek horrific as it plummeted toward me. I'd ditched my wheels and fled into the trees, figuring that would be the best place to lose it, but I was seriously regretting my decision now.

"Boyyyyyyyy!"

Goosebumps rippled along my arms as the voice hissed through the woods.

"This is your final hour, Dylan Wylde. I've come to collect you."

I wasn't ready to die. I guessed no one ever was, but it still felt too soon. We had things to do... places to go. We were the Society of the Owl and the Wolf, protectors of the island. But now I was toast.

"Come out, come out, wherever you are!" The Reaper's voice was almost sing song in its mockery. Great, even Death was toying with me.

Toy...

A thought flashed across my muddled mind but before I could grasp it, it vanished. I was missing something... I knew that much, but my terror was clouding my judgement.

The whirring drew closer as the setting sun filled the woods with gloom, making the Reaper's pulsing eyes stand out even clearer. It wound through the trunks toward me, its scythe swinging in its bony white hand.

I jumped up, fled into a clearing, and ducked as the Reaper swooped at me. Its shadow trailed over the ground as I pressed my face into the pine needles and dirt. Then it slowed, the hem of its black cloak swinging just ahead of me.

It was waiting, daring me to glance up. I almost did. Part of me wanted to get a closer look, to figure out if I was missing something, but my terror was too much. My arms and legs trembled as I pushed myself up and ran on, the whirring sound at my back, the scythe's shadow arcing across the ground toward me.

Chapter Two

"Boyyyyyyyy!"

The Reaper was at my back! I leaped toward a fallen log, slipped, slapped my hand against a tree trunk, and raced on.

Silence fell.

Had I lost it? I gazed up. My heart froze. It hung in the air, turning this way and that, as it searched for me. And then its arm creaked up and a bony white finger pointed right at me. *"There you are, boyyyyyyyy!"*

It swept down, its cloak cracking like a flag in a hurricane.

"Your moment's arrived, Dylan. I'm here to take you with me."

"Where?" My voice trembled madly.

"To the other side." A sly grin crept over its cadaverous face. *"And I don't mean the mainland."*

"I... I don't want to go."

"Of course you don't. No one ever does, Dylan. I wish it wasn't so, I wish I could grant you a long life, but alas, your time is up." Its eyes blazed like pools of lava as it drew closer, its scythe raised to strike me down.

"What are you doing?" It was Mom's voice... had it come from the Reaper?

"Nothing!" I heard Jamie reply before the sound cut out. I looked around, expecting to find them standing there in the woods. Maybe they'd come to pay their last respects.

There was no one there. I was alone with the Reaper.

Fear gave way to confusion as I stared at the creature and it stared back. Somehow it was less sinister now it wasn't speaking or moving, but I could still hear that weird hum.

"Hello?" I said. I felt my face burning red. Why was I being so polite? That thing was about to take me to Hades, or Valhalla, or who knew where? Maybe heaven, maybe hell, I had no idea. Anything seemed possible, anything except me managing to stay alive for much longer...

The Reaper remained silent. I almost stepped toward it. I was missing something, but I couldn't figure out what. And then its eyes flashed, and it hissed. Terror struck me. I turned and ran, smack into a tree. Bark bit the side of my face and a hollow crack rang in my ears. My legs gave out and I landed hard on the ground.

I rubbed my head and glanced back as the Reaper watched me. Slowly, I climbed to my feet and backed away, waiting for it to lunge, but it remained stock still. As I slunk from its field of vision, I expected its head to turn or its eyes to follow me, but they didn't.

It was like it was... frozen?

"I'm going," I said, still rubbing the side of my face. My cheek felt hot, gritty and numb, and it seemed I most likely had a headache in the mail. "Did you hear me?" Maybe if I sounded like I had places to be, it would buzz off and give me a few more years to live. Maybe it would forget me altogether...

I walked through the trees, forcing myself not to hurry, glancing back to see if it was following. It wasn't.

Finally, I stumbled from the brush back onto the road. My bike lay where I'd left it. I picked it up and wheeled it toward the house. Everything felt unreal, dreamlike. Nightmarish.

Jamie and Marshall strode down the lane toward me. Marshall's craggy face glowed as he stared down at the black box clasped in his hands. What was it? I could just make out a screen and radial stick. Jamie nodded to me. A twisted smile spread over his lips and he gave me that stupid super-villain laugh. "Here he is!"

Marshall giggled but his dead eyes were still glued to the box. And then I saw the antenna sticking up from the side and realized what it was...

The Island Scaregrounds is out now!

THE DAY OF THE JACKALOPE IS
NOW AVAILABLE ON AUDIBLE!

You've read the book, now experience the adventure in audio. Each of the characters have been brought to life in an entirely new way by the fabulously talented narrator J. Scott Bennett. Visit https://eldritchblack.com/audio-books to hear a sample now!

AFTERWORD

Thank you for reading The Day of the Jackalope! I hope you enjoyed the story. If you have a moment, I'd deeply appreciate a quick online review, even a sentence or two would be hugely helpful to pass on the word!

All the best,
Eldritch

ABOUT THE AUTHOR

Eldritch Black is an author of dark, whimsical spooky tales. His first novel 'The Book of Kindly Deaths' was published in 2014, and since then he's written a number of novels including 'The Day of The Jackalope', 'Krampus and The Thief of Christmas' & 'The Clockwork Magician'.

Eldritch was born in London, England and now lives in the United States in the woods on a small island that may or may not be called Weirdbey Island. When he isn't writing, Eldritch enjoys collecting ghosts, forgotten secrets and lost dreams.

Connect with Eldritch here:
www.eldritchblack.com
eldritch@eldritchblack.com

Made in USA - North Chelmsford, MA
1280532_9781077702530
01.14.2022 1123